Deadly Daughter

Book 3 of the Masterson Files

By

Andrew Allen Smith

Deadly Daughter

Dedication

Dedicated to the fans I never knew I had, and all the people who believe a dream can become a reality. If you believe in something enough, you can make it happen. Thank you for all the kind words that made me find my words.

Prologue

The bar was a seedy joint in the west side of Cincinnati, Ohio. It had the reputation for being full of overly tough people with nothing much to do but be overly tough. As Abby approached the bar, she saw Michael's car parked to the side and knew he would be in there somewhere. She wanted this to be a real test, but he was still protective. In the back of her mind, she felt that was sweet.

The door to the bar was painted a dingy red, and the handle was an old wrought iron cast that could have been black once. Now it was worn away from overuse and a lack of attention. The rest of the door was covered with greasy handprints from people too lazy to wash their hands or too busy to care.

Abby took a breath and opened the door. As she walked in, her eyes adjusted to the darker light, and she saw the familiar line of pool tables and the old jukebox in the corner. Two old dartboards hung in another corner, but they looked as though they had not been used. Their chalkboards had numerous graffiti messages about people's mothers on them.

Abby walked to the bar, still scanning the room, until she found a man sitting in the corner sipping on what looked to be a beer. Dressed in all black and more than a little wrinkled, she knew it was Michael. Abby wished he was not here. She needed to do this on her own.

It was Michael who, only a few days ago, had told Abby he would protect her for all their lives. She had laughed at him and asked what made him think she needed his help. He had laughed too but said he wanted to help her. Michael was always like that. Abby smiled to herself remembering how he had backpedaled, and she had let him, trying not to be an ass, but in the end, she said,

"Okay, I will prove it."

Michael had finally agreed to let Abby "clear a bar", and he would just watch in case things got out of hand. She was at first upset, but she finally agreed since it was possible that someone would pull a gun, even against a girl. She had looked at Michael with a little indignation and said, "I have trained as long as you," and he had smiled and nodded.

After looking around and watching police reports, Michael had helped Abby pick this bar, far enough away from home, but close enough for an easy drive.

Abby asked for a drink and the bartender leaned down to her and said, "You here alone, little gal? You should probably go somewhere else."

"I asked for a beer," Abby said, now lost in the moment and oblivious to what was, in her mind, a rite of passage.

"Yes, ma'am," the bartender said, and gave her a Budweiser bottle.

"Maybe you need to dance," a voice came from behind. Abby turned and saw Michael was watching though he did not move. He sat sipping his drink and she wondered again if there was any alcohol in it. The man in front of her was about 6'4 and weighed well over 300 pounds. His clothes were worn and ragged and his face unshaven.

"Nope," Abby said. "My card is full." She then spun around and looked back at the bartender. Abby stood 5'4" and was barely 110 pounds. She worked out often, but she looked diminutive against just about anyone. Her long blonde hair was currently in a ponytail, but it was usually worn around her shoulder with amazing curls that just looked perfect in every way. She looked young but was as old as Michael. Abby's lithe and crisp features were a testament to years of hard work keeping herself in shape.

Abby watched in the mirror as the giant man moved forward. She also saw in the mirror that Michael did not move, it was time to trust and to believe he would not interfere. After all, he promised and to Michael a promise meant more than just words. She felt the man put a calloused hand on her shoulder, and with a casual defiance she reached back and grabbed just the thumb. Twisting it, she turned as she forced him down, bringing all her strength on just that digit.

"You must be from Ohio," Abby said. "I was clear I did not want to dance. I suppose momma' never taught you what 'no' meant. Did she pop your cherry or something? I have heard you people in Ohio do stuff like that."

The giant man was whimpering a little, trying to grab his hand, but Abby was very nearly breaking bone as she held his thumb tightly. The joint was just not meant to bend that way.

Abby heard chairs scoot back, screeching like a whine from two plates being pressed together and rubbed back and forth, and then heard a voice say, "Let him go, woman."

Abby turned but did not change her grip. "Or what?" she said defiantly.

"Or I will make you," a smaller man said, as he stepped forward. "That submission crap won't work on me. You best just let him go and move your Ohio hating ass out of here."

Abby pushed the large man's hand down and let go and there was a pop. The man grabbed his hand, and as he looked up, Abby kicked him in the chest with a front kick that would have made Bruce Lee proud. He fell backwards, still clutching his hand

and now gasping for air.

The smaller man jumped forward much faster than Abby would have guessed. She still had the advantage of distance though, and as he reached for her, she simply ducked under, and he slammed into the bar. "There's a bar there," Abby said as she moved away.

The man swung back at her and charged, but Abby once again slid sideways, this time while pushing her leg out, tripping the man and watching him fall on a table, then over a chair. "There's a table there," Abby said leaning forward at him, "and a chair too."

Two more men ran at Abby, and she was quickly surrounded. Her original assailant had stood up, and though his hand was being favored, he looked more than a little upset. The second man had recovered and was a little less aggressive, which meant he would be thinking things out. The other two men were pressing forward, and Abby decided to feign for them. She moved forward, and they fell back, not sure why she was coming for them so aggressively. At the last second, she turned to her first attacker and hit him in the face. As she reached up, she also grabbed his thumb again, twisting it a little more. He fell to the ground for a moment, holding it. Taking advantage of her split attention, the second man pressed in and grabbed Abby from behind. As he pushed her towards the bar, she put her feet out, found purchase and pushed back hard, flying over him as she did so. Her flip took him by surprise, and he fell forward. Being a nice woman, Abby helped him fall face first into the bar.

"The bar is still there," Abby said as he tried to get up.

The last two men who had joined stopped for a moment, and Abby simply looked at them. They both moved back to a table with measured speed and sat down.

Abby picked up her beer and smiled to herself for a moment. She took a drink and looked in the mirror and saw Michael had not moved an inch during the entire ordeal.

The bartender looked at her with an unsure visage, "I had to call the police."

"I know, I heard you," Abby said. She reached into her pocket and pulled out a fifty-dollar bill. She placed it on the bar and said, "Thanks for the drink." As Abby walked to the door, several people glanced at her with a look that could be respect, then went back to their games or conversations. In this type of bar, it was usually better not to get involved. Abby looked back and saw the two men getting up as they tried to keep from adding to their obvious pain while their friends got up to help them. Abby was guarded because she wasn't out of the bar yet, but they didn't even look at her. The second man slapped at one of the others as they tried to help him up.

As Abby walked by the man in black, she smiled at Michael. He sat there silently, watching everyone. She was proud of herself but had observed Michael in a bar as well. He always tried to defuse things first, but when there was a fight, well, he was very quick. Michael liked to quote many people and often said the best fighter was the one who did not fight. Abby felt good about her passage, but it had been a lot of hard work. Abby had sparred with Michael for weeks to prepare herself before coming here, and it was obvious to her he held back. She knew that after today he would give her a little more leeway. After all, she was a general's daughter, and she deserved the respect.

As Abby walked outside, she breathed in the cool air and smiled. She walked to her car and got in. She felt good. It was not good to hurt people, but she let it happen. It was not good to be aggressive unless you had to, but she did not start anything. It was not good to be deadly, but she knew she was her father's daughter, and her father was one of the deadliest people in the world. She smiled again and thought, "And then there is Michael, in a league of his own, and perhaps even deadlier than her father." Abby was happy with herself though, for she had found out today that she could hold her own in a rough situation, and that is exactly what she wanted. It would get her the thing she wanted even more, respect.

Chapter 1

Abby drove the jet-black Suburban around the side of the house and watched the reinforced garage door lumber upwards. Inside, another car sat under its blanket, along with a variety of motor vehicles meant for play and beyond. As usual, the garage was spotless. There wasn't a single speck of dust to be found, and the steel cabinets on the walls, which housed a variety of tools, could have been purchased and mounted yesterday.

Abby got out of the giant Suburban. She held her coffee as she walked to the back of the car and removed a small bag of groceries from the trunk. It was not difficult to work with as she had her purse slung over her body, so she simply skipped to the back of the garage to a whimsical tune only she could hear.

As Abby approached the door of the house it clicked and whirred. The electronic locks that Michael had added sensed her phone and unlocked at her approach. She thought it was a bit unnerving to consider the phone was her key, but Michael explained that her key would still work as well. This lock system would be able to track who got in, who got out, and enable them to be safer. Other girlfriends would have considered their boyfriend paranoid, or a little crazy, just for thinking they needed to be tracked so efficiently, but Abby had been with Michael for a long time. Since college they had been friends, and after Michael had been cast aside by an ex-girlfriend, they had started seeing each other. First, they were friends and then as a couple that everyone should try to be. Abby and Michael shared a passion for each other that most people don't ever get to experience in their lives. A passion for life, a passion for love, and a passion for each other.

When Michael's mother had died, Michael became more driven. Even though he was well off before, he found a dispassionate side to himself that only Abby seemed to truly understand. She introduced Michael to her father, a General, and he took advantage of this time in Michael's life and used him, for what he believed was protecting the United States Government. Michael eliminated a significant number of people that were enemies of the state, and in the process made an even more significant amount of money. The house he and Abby were in was but one of the homes Michael owned, along with the property around it, and quite a bit more. To many it would seem extravagant or wasteful. To Michael only Abby was important, and he could give up anything for her.

Abby smiled as she opened the door into the large lower level. There was a gym and a big sparring area. Behind a false wall was Michael's room. He barely used it anymore, but inside were the tools of his trade and the technology to be able to communicate with others in a rapid manner. Abby was used to all of this because her father was a General in a covert group that handled "problems." The group didn't even have a designation, and there was no recruitment, nor an easy way out. It was something that was necessary, but not popular. It was something people wanted there to protect them but didn't want to ever acknowledge. Abby had known her father was involved in a great deal, but it was only after she began dating Michael that she realized how deep it went.

Abby walked into the lower level, stopped and looked in a mirror. She was not a tall woman, only five four, but she was fiery and had proven herself over and over, to herself, to her father, and to Michael. To Michael it had never mattered. He considered himself her protector and would have loved her no matter what she did. Though it was many years ago when Abby had proven that she could handle things herself, Michael still vowed to keep her safe. Her father was similar. The General would and had sent people to protect Abby even though he knew that she could protect herself. Michael was more casual about it though. He would let her take care of herself until he saw that he needed to step in, which was a very rare occurrence. Of all the people in the world Abby could be around, she always felt safe with Michael. She believed he felt the same.

As Abby continued to look at herself in the mirror, she noted her long blond hair in a ponytail and her slim body clad in casual jeans and cowboy boots. Her figure would have been model worthy if she was not so small, and her eyes glistened in the reflection. They were crystal blue and said to be mesmerizing. Michael told her often that he was captivated by those very eyes. Abby closed them then for a moment and thought of Michael, his rugged handsome features. Michael was muscular and exuded power, and his eyes glistened as hers did. When he looked into her eyes all was right with the world.

"Michael," Abby said as she climbed the stairs, "I'm home!" Abby loved their home. The stairs opened to a view made in heaven, a rugged one of the hills of Dubois, Wyoming. The house was set perfectly to watch over the land below, and from the main room anyone could watch the sun rise each day. Michael said that it gave him hope as he watched the sun climb into the skies. Abby knew it also reminded him of his mother, long since gone, but never forgotten to him.

"Michael!" Abby yelled again as she walked to the kitchen. She looked around but saw nothing, listening she heard nothing. The house was quiet except for her voice.

Abby set down the groceries and pulled out her cell phone and dialed a number. Almost instantly, she heard Michael's phone ringing in the bedroom. Abby hung up her phone and took the purse off her shoulder. Setting it all down on the stylish couch she walked towards the bedroom.

"Michael!" Abby yelled one more time, "Are you here?"

There was no sound coming from anywhere. The house was quiet as a tomb, with silence being an unusual norm. Michael usually had music blaring in the background as he worked. Abby considered for a moment. She had left just after breakfast and he would have worked out and maybe worked in the garage then, probably followed by a shower. Abby thought about it and knew that was probably it. Michael was in the shower.

Abby walked down the long hallway and didn't hear a shower, nor anything else. As she turned the corner though, she saw a towel on the floor and clothes scattered. It was a good sign. "Michael," she said as she rounded the corner. Again, nothing. The overly large bathroom was empty, as was the bedroom. The clothes on the floor and the wet towel were there, but Michael was not. Abby started to get concerned.

Abby walked with purpose into the bathroom and looked in the shower. It was still wet. The floor was covered with water and glancing back in the bedroom, she saw his towel laying crumpled on the floor she traced the steps. The wall of the shower had not been squeegeed yet which Michael did every time. The floors still had traces of water on them, yet Michael always wiped the floor and hung the towels also, letting them air dry and allowing him to reuse them a time or two. He kept things neat, almost too neat. Something was wrong.

Abby walked back into the room and yelled louder, "Michael!" She dialed his phone again and this time heard it near-by and saw the phone's light under the bed. She fell to her knees and reached far under the bed to grab the phone, then stood up, hanging up her phone. She stared at it. It was clean and crisp as always, with a picture of the two of them on the screen, her long blonde curls hanging down her shoulders and him with his arm enveloping her. She smiled for a moment, but only a moment, as she walked to the next bedroom.

Abby found nothing out of place in the second bedroom or the second bathroom, but as she opened the door to the third bedroom the wind blew across her face. The window was open in the room that overlooked the hills below. She walked over to it and looked down, and below her a rope dangled with tight climbing knots. It was then she heard a noise behind her. Abby spun to face a man in a black suit coming at her, arms wide.

Abby did not scream or yelp or do anything that the man may have expected. Instead, she charged too. The room was large but they both crossed it like two rams heading towards each other, and at the last moment Abby dropped to the floor and smashed the man's knee with her boot. He screamed in pain but reached back for her and grabbed her hair. Abby's ponytail was a weakness for her as the man pulled her down hard to the ground with it. She did not stop as she fell but instead rounded her back and did a reverse summersault, rolling over the man's hand. Startled, he let go, but as she passed, her boots were now over his hands, and she stomped hard with the heel onto both of them.

Again, the man screamed. Abby did not slow down, nor did she even pause. She spun around and kicked up into the man's covered face. There was a loud crack, and she knew she had broken his jaw.

Michael had always told Abby that there were lots of types of people, but the only ones he ever worried about in a fight were the ones that got madder with pain. You could shoot them, kick them in the groin, or even cut off portions of their body, and they just did not seem to notice. This man was acting like that as he screamed a gurgled noise and redoubled his efforts, reaching and swinging for Abby like a wild man.

Abby wasn't worried about the man. She kept her cool, controlling the situation and when he grabbed for her, she fell on the side of his arm with all the force she could muster. Abby felt his elbow joint break. It was a hard snap and as Abby pulled away the arm dangled uselessly to the side of him. He could not stand, but still bellowed in anger and pain, rocking back and forth in her direction. Abby looked to the wall and saw the small shelf. She quickly ran to it and grabbed "Iacocca, An Autobiography" from a long stack of books. As the man struggled and grimaced in pain crawling towards her, she opened the front page of the book and took out the Walther PPK from inside. Pointing the weapon at the man's face, Abby simply said, "Stop."

The man looked at the gun that Abby was pointing at him and was aware it was not shaking at all. He stopped crawling and looked up at the tiny powerhouse. "Ya brak mah jaah," he said almost unintelligibly.

"Where is Michael?" she demanded.

"Goaane," the man said.

"Take off the mask," Abby said pointedly. As the man did so, she realized she had done significant damage to him. His jaw hung loose to one side and was obviously very painful, and very broken. His eye was black and bleeding, and his arm dangled at an angle not easily done by contortionists, let alone normal people. "Where is Michael?" Abby repeated.

"Goaannneee," the man said again, and as his voice trailed, the sound of the 380 going off echoed in the room. Abby had aimed and shot him in the calf of his left leg. The man groaned in pain, but his mouth did not let it sound like more than a whale's bellow in the ocean.

"Let's start over," Abby said with a calm voice. "I am betting you know who I am, but I don't know you. It appears that you are trespassing in my home. I think you are saying that Michael, one of

15

the homeowners, is gone. Let's play a game. I will ask a question and you will answer. Nod if you understand."

The man looked at Abby and nodded, slowly.

"You were here to take Michael, right?" Abby asked the man, and he nodded. Then Abby asked, "Someone else was with you?"

The man nodded again and then Abby asked him, "The person has taken Michael?"

The man sat for a moment. Abby shot the gun again, this time hitting him in the calf of his right leg. The man began rapidly nodding yes as he clutched his leg. Abby looked at him and saw that he was done, there was no fight left in him. "That was really loud, and my ears are ringing like crazy. God, if the TV shows were for real, all the damn TV cops would be deaf from firing without ear protection." She smiled a little. Abby was in control.

The man tried to smile but his jaw was less than functional. "I bet that hurts," Abby said.

The man nodded with eagerness this time and Abby asked him, "Was this government?"

The man looked at Abby and shook his head no. "Puhhbuck," he said.

Abby struggled with the word and cocked her head a little. "Payback?" she asked the man, and he nodded. Abby stood for a moment and realized that she had the pistol in one hand, the book in the other. The man was quivering and would probably pass out from shock soon. He was bleeding from his face, his hand, two bullet holes, and probably internally in his arm. Abby dropped the book and picked up her phone and dialed 911. As she waited, she thought for a moment and then hung up. Quickly she looked through her phone and dialed another number.

"Hello," came a deep voice.

"I need some help," Abby said.

"You okay?" asked the voice.

"No, it's bad," Abby said calmly.

"I will be right there," returned the voice.

The man on the floor looked up at Abby as his adrenaline waned. She pointed the gun at him, and he was aware her aim did not move a millimeter. For that reason, he did not move. He was getting white as he sat there losing more blood, but Abby knew better than to get close or give him an opening. She was 100 pounds lighter, so even as good as she was, she could lose.

Abby heard a gallop and in a moment two giant dogs bounded into the room. They ran over and sniffed her while keeping a wary eye on her guest. The man on the floor, if not white before, surely turned white now. The dogs were formidable and walked around the room smelling their surroundings. If it were not bad enough, a giant then entered, spotted Abby and went over to her.

The huge man looked at Abby and the pistol in her hand, then at the man on the floor. "Well, I guess you are okay, but did you run the car up here and run over him?" he asked her.

Abby giggled, and the man made a grimace. Abby then stood up, a second wind coming to her after the adrenaline low. She clicked the safety on the pistol, putting it in her belt. "Michael is gone," she said quietly.

Alan glanced at Abby then knelt down to the man and looked him in the eye. "Damn, she did a number on you! You will need more than I can do, but I will stop the bleeding."

The man seemed nervous as Alan tossed him about effortlessly, checking his wounds. "Bullets went through, no issue. This arm is a mess, and his hand has a few tendons popped," he stated. Alan then looked down at the man's face. "This must hurt like hell." The man rolled his eyes. "Your jaw is not broken, just dislocated. Alan grabbed his head in a massive hand. This might smart," Alan said as he worked the man's jaw around then popped it into place with a quick twist. The pop sounded gruesome, but it had the desired effect. The man looked better as it held its place. He screamed inside his mouth as Alan pulled his hand away from his head. The pain hit him wave after wave. Alan said to him in a serious tone, "I would skip talking for a while. I know it hurts."

Abby spoke, "He indicated someone took Michael for revenge or payback or something."

Alan smiled. "That true?" he asked the man.

The man nodded again with an eagerness that was deliberate, looking at Abby.

Alan smiled. "Well, I know it is hard for you to communicate, but you need to tell me who you are and where Michael was taken. We have some options. I can pop your jaw in and out all night, let the dogs play tug-o-war with your legs, or let Abby have her way with you. Any of that sound good?"

The man shook his head no at Alan.

"So how do we proceed?" Alan asked the man. The man pointed to the window and Alan looked over. "You need to show me something?" he asked, and the man nodded. Alan easily picked up the man by the front of his shirt, allowing him the little mobility he had with his short, shot up legs. They went over to the window and looked out and the man pointed to the hills beyond.

"Where?" Alan said, and the man again pointed to the hills. Alan leaned out the window a little and saw nothing. The man leaned out then, continuing to point, and as Alan kept looking, the man pushed back against him with whatever strength he had left. He then plummeted out the window to the hard ground. He hit with a sickening thud, 200 feet below.

Abby and Alan looked out of the window at the man's mangled body. Abby stepped back all the way inside and asked, "What now?

"I guess we look around," Alan said, as he threw the grapple down with the man and closed and locked the window. "Then it's time to find Michael," Alan said.

Chapter 2

Abby looked in the mirror as she stood in the guest bedroom. Her tussle with the unknown assailant had left her disheveled. She was also a bit frustrated as she wanted answers and the assailant had jumped to his death to prevent them from learning something. She thought to herself, "Why?" He had seemed to be cooperating.

Alan had sent the dogs down to the body as he proceeded to go there. Abby looked out the window and saw that the dogs were sitting like silent black statues in the lawn. They were waiting for their master who was hampered by the fact that he had only two legs and could not run at their speed. Abby looked around the room and began reviewing the area with careful precision. She was pretty sure there was no danger, but she thought that there had to have been a reason the man stayed. She knew there was something missing, or something was changed, or perhaps that she was a target as well.

Abby walked the path to her bedroom and looked in from the doorway. There were very few people who could take on Michael one on one, she thought. They must have caught him totally unaware. While she glanced around the room, she saw a strange pattern on the wall. It was nearly imperceptible, but she knew this house like, well, like she knew Michael. She walked towards the markings, and as she got nearer, she saw them. A line of very small objects, extremely difficult to make out. She stopped, looked closer, and was careful not to touch them as she examined the tiny darts. Each was less than a half of an inch long, with small flights, and they looked to be imbedded in the wall. As she continued to look, she saw that there were at least 100 of them in a wide pattern. It explained how they could have gotten Michael. They sprayed the area with darts for then they couldn't miss.

Abby looked at the walls while walking around the room. There were only two areas the small darts had imbedded in the wall, so only two short bursts. They must have gotten Michael as he got out of the shower, naked, or else he would have had the advantage, she thought. Abby walked through the room with care and scanned the floor almost a fiber at a time but did not see any darts. She then got on her knees and began inspecting the floor from only inches away, straining to see something, anything, but still she saw nothing. Abby now knew why the man had stayed. The area was in the process of being cleaned.

Abby stood and looked for anything that was being used to clean the area. She went to each room, and in the third bedroom she found a small cloth bag. The man must have hidden it there when he heard her come home and call for Michael. She was careful with the bag and opened it to see a significant number of darts, fibers, and a few other items. She gently closed it and examined that room, seeing nothing else.

Abby then walked to the kitchen and set the bag on the table. She went to the balcony and looked over to see Alan down with the body. She did not want to interrupt his concentration, so she went to the cabinets and got out some cloth gloves, tweezers and a few knives. She was about to dump the bag when she thought twice about it and instead headed to a hall closet. Opening it, she stretched to the top shelf and found a black pillowcase. She walked back to the kitchen table and spread out the pillowcase on it. Abby then took her time and poured the bag's contents on the covered table. Items fell out without a sound on the pillowcase, and they were easy to see in the bright sunlight that shone in the window. When the bag seemed to be empty, Abby turned it inside out and made sure. She then set the bag aside.

For a moment, Abby was astounded at the size of the darts. They were very tiny, and she wondered what type of weapon would fire them. Then she looked in a drawer and retrieved a pair of reading glasses. She had kept them from when she was making jewelry, knowing she might need them again. Sitting down at the table, Abby peered at the darts and studied them. She moved one off by itself with the tweezers. To her they looked like small Daisy dart gun darts. There were light black threads tailing a fine point, almost the size of an insulin needed. Abby turned them over and over. She was sure Michael would know who might make a weapon that shot this, but she did not. The other items in the bag included a few small cloths with blood on them, and a Kleenex. Abby was sure it may have meant something as well, but she would wait for Alan.

Abby folded the pillowcase over itself, keeping the contents covered, and then she set it aside. She put the tools and glasses on top of the pillowcase and got up thinking, then went to the kitchen for a moment and put away her groceries introducing some modicum of "normal". She was worried about Michael and was trying to consider her next move. There seemed to be no good answers and a lot of questions. She pressed herself to hold it together and think how Michael would solve this.

Michael had told Abby something once which she was straining to remember. It was such a weird conversation, but she did not want to let go of the thought. Michigan, Larry, it was all starting to pull together. A gun shop in central Michigan! It was one of the few places Michael would trust to find weapons for himself. Abby had not been to Michigan in a long time, but Michael would drive up there occasionally and bring back something new. He felt that there were only a few people he could trust in his line of business and Larry was one of them. Abby filed the thought away excitedly. She would ask Alan about it and perhaps he would know more, and then they could call or find out what is necessary.

Abby was feeling good about things and then realized that in her rush, the garage may still be open, so she needed to check the house over. She went to all of the rooms again and decided the upstairs seemed secure. There was little that could be found there without a bigger team and a lot of time. She had not gone back downstairs so did so now and looked over the spacious gym area. It appeared empty and untouched. She went to the weight rack and lifted three weights in sequence and the huge door clicked and slid slightly, allowing her to push it open. The lights began to come on, and Abby saw that this room was untouched. She slid the door closed, and immediately after slid the weights back into place. She was answered with a thick click as the door secured again.

Abby then went back to the garage. The Suburban door was closed but the garage door was still open. She was sure Alan would come back in, but she didn't want it to be unprotected. She thought for a second and decided to leave it for now. Nothing in the garage had looked out of place, but Abby did walk out to the road and look at tracks. She could not be sure, but it looked like there was another tire print besides hers. She wished she had paid more attention to her class in forensics but laughed because she knew that she had done well. It just was not used often and that was a long time ago.

Smiling, Abby went back in the house and walked upstairs to wait for Alan. She knew she was in control of herself.

Chapter 3

Alan examined the body carefully. The first thing he did was check for a pulse. The fall was almost two hundred feet, but that was not certain death, just very likely death. Though the odd tilt of the body seemed to indicate the man was dead, after checking a few places, Alan nodded his head, concluding to himself that the man was actually dead.

Alan began looking for answers by rolling the man to his side, checking all pockets and emptying them on the ground. Normally he would have been more careful as he had been years ago on the force, but now he needed answers quickly.

Alan looked up at the window and was a little baffled as to why the man killed himself. He was almost cooperating when the man had pushed past him and fallen out of the window. There seemed to be no reason for the act except for the fact that Alan and Abby were about to get rough.

The man's pocket contents were as helpful as the lint in them. Not much to go on and nothing that seemed to lead anywhere. Alan then began checking everywhere for any type of ID. It seemed there were no visible signs of identification, no dog tags, no nothing. Alan opened the man's mouth then. The dental records may get an ID, but that would take time and some type of agency involvement. Still drawing a blank here.

One of Alan's amazing dogs came over to the body and began sniffing his face, then looked at Alan and sniffed the man's ear. Alan looked at the man, and at his ear, and finally saw what his dog already knew. A tiny earbud was lodged deep inside. This was truly a high-tech piece of equipment if it was that small, but Alan needed to see it. Reaching into his pocket, he pulled out a Black Tinker Swiss Army Knife. After that he pulled out a pair of small tweezers from the case and used them to carefully reach into the man's ear. It was patient work, for every time he pulled on the small buds they seemed to retract back into the man's ear.

After a few minutes, Alan was able to get the necessary leverage with the tweezers and the small blade of the knife to pull out the earbud. It was tiny, and Alan was impressed with its molding. If the man had been alive, it would have hurt like hell pulling it out. Alan flipped it over gently and one of the dogs looked at the bud and cocked his head slightly. Alan lowered his head to the earbud and heard the light whining, or was that talking? He tried to strain to hear but realized that the bud would be much louder in the inner ear.

Alan looked down at the broken man laying before him and knew he would not be going anywhere. Closing his hand around the bud, he walked up the hill to the front of the house to talk to Abby and see if they could use this newfound clue. As he did, the two dogs bounded behind him, once again making it to the top of the hill far before he could get there.

As Alan topped the hill, the two dogs galloped around with playful grace for a moment until he looked at them. Then like scorned children, the dogs fell in next to him. Alan walked to the open garage and went in the house, walked upstairs and found Abby waiting.

"I found something," Alan told Abby.

"Me too," Abby said.

Alan laughed a little, then started. He pulled out the small earbud and laid it on the table. "I am betting our friend didn't want to jump, but something was said that made him do so. I am also pretty sure they heard everything we said."

"How about now?" Abby asked. "Can they hear us now?"

"Possibly," Alan said, "but I am betting it requires bone induction." Walking over to the cabinets, he went through a couple of them and found some tin foil. He then walked over to the table and made a big wrapping ball of it which he put the earbud in. "Won't hear anything now," Alan said. "I can take it to the house and see what it has in it and who it is transmitting to," Alan grinned, "I would rather not put it in my ear."

Abby nodded to Alan. She barely knew this giant, but he had helped them before, and she trusted him. She then unfolded the pillowcase. "I am betting these were shot at Michael while he was getting out of the shower. The window would've been open for them to get to him because he likes the breeze," Abby stated. "I am not sure what they actually are, what fires them, or how they would have taken him out though. Michael knew a guy in Michigan, a Larry or something or other, who knows more about weapons than anyone. He told me about him when we were watching a Mark Wahlberg movie. There was some guy talking about shooting and stuff and Michael said, "That sounds like Larry." He then said he had bought a few things from him, and he was one of the few gunsmiths that he actually trusted."

"I know of Larry. I know how to get in touch with him too," Alan said, as he rolled one of the darts around on the pillowcase. "I will try to contact him then come back over if you need me. Are you ok? Do you want to go with me?" Alan asked Abby.

Abby smiled and said, "I'll make some calls. I am fine."

Alan smiled back. "Melody would love this."

Abby smiled again. "Where is Melody? Oh, and glad my tragedy can be your playground."

Alan smirked. "Sorry, I know this is tough. We will find Michael. If they are using darts, they want him for something. We will find him, or he will find a way out."

Abby hugged herself for a moment. "Yeah, I know. It's just that I would never have expected..."

Alan broke in. "Everyone can be taken off guard. You know that, so did Michael. They had to know him pretty well to know how to get to him. Oh, and Mel is off in DC somewhere. Alex keeps her busy, but she gets here often. I don't want to call her unless you want me too, because you know she will tell Alex and the group, and she'll tell your dad."

"Don't say anything until we know a little more," Abby told Alan.

"I'll be back. I will let one of the dogs stay in the area," Alan said.

"Thanks," Abby said as Alan went downstairs. She went to a small monitor on the kitchen counter that showed the garage. As Alan left, she pressed a button, and the door began to close. Abby watched with disassociated fascination as the complex locking mechanisms fell into place and the door sealed. Every contingency had been considered. As the multiple lock points snapped into place Abby realized she was safe, or at least as safe as Michael was a few hours ago.

Chapter 4

There was pain. Michael slowly tried to open his eyes as he sampled the metallic taste of blood on his lips. He stopped, closed his eyes, relaxed his body and stayed still. Listening, Michael knew he was in a vehicle. He was rolling from side to side on hard steel. He deduced it must be a panel van or something similar. He knew if he opened his eyes or seemed awake, he would be seen. Michael did not want that, so he continued to listen with his eyes closed.

The ground below the van was rhythmic, clickity, clickity, click. Michael figured out that it was a concrete road, somewhere on a large stretch, as he was not wavering much.

Michael felt his hands tied behind his back. The bonds were tight, most likely handcuffs. He felt his legs and moved them only slightly with the next bump. They were bound as well, but he could not discern the type of binding.

Michael listened. He heard no voices, no talking, not even music. He took a chance and opened his eyes quickly then relaxed them again. The brief flash let him know he was in a white interior panel van. That meant nothing. It could have been any van at all, from a black van on the outside to an exterminator van. In the end, it was not of any help.

Michael thought of Abby then. Was she ok, was anything wrong with her? Anger flashed in him, but he restrained that anger as he needed more information. Michael flashed his eyes open again. The back of the truck was a standard panel van door. If he could undo the latch, he could release himself. He lightly tested his bonds again, and his fingers for movement.

"He's awake again," Michael heard a deep voice say. He didn't feel the dart hit him. Darkness descended on Michael, and as he faded, he thought of Abby.

Chapter 5

Alan walked into his home with one dog trotting next to him. The sleek modern design was more than pleasing to him with the bright white walls, cool stone, and the angular corners that made the rooms seem inviting but crisp.

The large one-story home was built into the side of a hill and partially underground, much like Alan had found Michael's to be. The difference was no stairs. Alan did not work out in a traditional sense. He ran, played with the dogs, cut his own wood and was overly active, all outdoors. Michael liked to spar inside in his gym. Alan would rather run with the dogs and let them take him where they may. It was a very different way to the same end.

Alan walked into his spacious den where a computer with four monitors surrounded him. He reached into his pocket and got out the ball of tinfoil and unwrapped the earpiece. Taking a small device from a shelf, he put it by the earpiece and typed on his computer. In a few moments the device identified the frequency the earpiece was transmitting on. Alan then typed a few more keys and watched as the system began mimicking the modulation. He hit a switch on his screen and the volume came on.

"In route. He woke again but we put him back out," Alan heard a voice say on the speakers. Alan hit another button and a light lit up and started blinking red. He was recording the transmissions.

"Secondary target is in the home still, observing," the voice continued.

Alan thought it was sloppy not to have such a high-tech earpiece encrypted, but to encrypt may have taken more power or caused other issues. He set the thought aside.

"The interferer has left the area. He is not in sight at this time. We can proceed with the collection of the second target," the voice continued.

"If you fail like Max, you will be treated like Max. Make sure this happens. Her capture will ensure the primaries cooperation," a second voice said.

Alan opened another program on a different monitor and watched a series of concentric circles lay over top of a map. He had three antennas in the valley to allow him to track the dogs when they were out of range. They were rapidly recalibrated to look for the headset's signal. The circles started to converge on two points. One ended up being at his house and the other was near Abby. He let a map slide over the images, and it stopped on a hill about a half mile from Michael's house.

Alan opened another box on the shelf and pulled out a small headset. Typing a few commands on the screen, he could suddenly hear the messages on his headset.

"Execution in 10," the voice said.

"Good. Report directly after," said the second voice.

Alan knew it was nearly 6 miles to Abby and Michael's house. It would take him more than 10 minutes to get there. Alan clicked his tongue, and his giant dog was by his side. He left the systems on, walked out of the room, and let the door lock behind him as he ran to Michael and Abby's house. He would not let her be taken. Even though he knew that she could take care of herself, he was not willing to take that chance. As he ran, he dialed Abby.

"Hello," Abby answered the phone.

"No talking, 9 minutes, be prepped. Call the dog to you," Alan said.

"Come here," Abby said to the dog. He came over to her and looked at Abby as she held the phone out. The dog seemed to know what to do and listened.

Alan said a simple word on the phone, "Protect."

The dog walked away from the phone toward the door, paced backwards a few steps, then lay on the floor watching the door.

Abby put her phone to her ear. "See you soon." She heard Alan pant and then there was silence.

Chapter 6

Abby was not waiting. She ran downstairs to the exercise room and moved the weights again. She felt the door click and slide ajar, and she pushed it open in a frenzy. As she walked in, the bright white lights powered on and the computers in the corner whirred with excitement. Abby went to the larger drawers and slid the top one open. There, Michael's P90 and FN57 waited patiently.

Abby took the Walther from her belt and laid it on Michael's desk, then walked to another drawer and opened it to find a series of tactical belts. She pulled one out made just for her and locked it into place. Next to the FN57 was a holster, which Abby grabbed and mounted on her belt along with a pouch for two magazines. She then opened the drawer beneath the pistol and rifle and pulled out two magazines for each of the weapons. Abby considered for a moment. That would be over 140 shots for whatever came at her. She assumed that would be fine. She also knew Alan would be there soon.

Abby started thinking a million different things at once when she suddenly thought of Michael. They had been talking when he first discussed with her what he did. She had asked him, *"Aren't you afraid of getting shot or losing sometime?"* She remembered *Michael telling her, "Most people in a tense situation are so worried about what they forgot that they forget why they are there. When I am in a tense situation, my goal is only to eliminate that situation. I use the tools I have, and at the top of the list is inner calm. If I can disassociate myself from the chaos, my calm will always prevail, and my shots will be true. I just need to make sure my opponents stay in the chaos and can't see me as clearly as I see them."*

At first, the thought of Michael had threatened to undermine Abby, but now it gave her clarity, and she knew what she had to do. She put the magazines on her belt and walked to another drawer. Inside, she grabbed two "flashbangs". The light and sound grenades would disorient anyone if she needed to use them. She then opened another drawer and pulled out a twelve-inch survival knife.

Abby saw the light behind her and looked to her side. The screens on the wall were now lit up. One with computer information and a series of others with cameras in the perimeter. Abby knew all of the cameras were well hidden and both regular and infrared capable. Because it was daylight, the camera would find people easily, and they would track based on motion and facial recognition.

As Abby gazed at the cameras, she was happy there was no one on them right now. She smiled, for she had the advantage. To the side of the monitors was a small panel and one of the buttons noted lockdown. She hit it and saw a series of green lights come on one by one. The garage door was reinforced and would handle anything that came at it. The back door was 200 feet in the air, and the front door was built by Michael's own design. Michael had said it would take a tank to get through it, but it had never been tested. The walls were all reinforced. Michael had laughed at all the houses that put in great doors but standard walls, making entry easy. Every wall had extra reinforcement and was quite bulletproof. All of the windows were bullet resistant, and it would take a lot to get through them. Michael had said his 50 might penetrate, but it would not be lethal afterward unless several shots hit the same place.

All of the lights on the panel were green, and Abby knew she could hold out for quite a while, but she needed someone to start on the trek to Michael, and to understand who had taken him and why.

Red lights clicked on and Abby looked at her watch. It was

10 minutes since Alan had warned her, and now she saw the men moving up. She counted three coming from different angles. The cameras locked on each of them, zoomed and began running recognition, but they all had on a full-face mask. There would likely be no matches with the minimal amount of data that was being collected.

Abby continued to look at what the cameras were seeing. She saw that the first man reached the front door and the second man got to the garage. The third man began climbing up the balcony by a rope thrown over the edge. Abby watched patiently as the men checked and rechecked their watches and spoke to each other, probably through earbuds similar to the one Alan had taken off the body still laying below.

Cameras tracked and changed angles, and in the process, different views came online as they tracked the same three people. Abby decided the easiest choice was to handle the one on the balcony first.

Abby ran upstairs into the spacious den and hit the remote. The screens popped on, and then she hit a button and suddenly all the camera angles were online. Abby waited for a moment, then seeing the rope on the monitor, she opened the door and looked down as the man climbed upwards. He was about 100 feet off the ground and had about 100 feet left to go. Abby considered and decided it would be cruel to make this last too long, but then she rethought and remembered the earbuds. She waited as he climbed and reached the ledge, then she stepped out into view. Abby grabbed the rope and her knife and looked at the man saying, "Shhh," as she held the knife inches from the bindings holding him. A flick of the wrist and he would fall to his death.

"She is here," the man said as he reached for the balcony, but Abby was quicker. The rope cut like a piece of thread being sliced by a katana and the man fell. As Abby went back inside, she heard a sickening thud from below. Once inside Abby locked the door. Checking her screens she saw the red turn to green. The house was once again secure. What Abby saw next amazed her.

Shiva was in view. Alan's dog had been left and told to protect. Abby had once seen the dogs in action with some guys who were trying to take her and some friends, but she was not ready for what was going on now. The dog was silent, and it was obvious that the man at the garage was completely unaware. He was a big guy, probably 6 feet and at least 220 pounds. Shiva was a German Shepherd and probably weighed about 100 pounds. As the dog advanced, the man stood oblivious. He was probably talking to the other man as his mouth was moving, but Abby had no sound. He was not holding his weapon up either. Shiva grabbed the man by the back of the ankle so quickly he probably didn't feel it. The attack made him crumple immediately. Abby guessed the dog had ripped out his Achilles tendon. As the man fell hard, he grabbed his weapon, however Shiva had not stopped his attack. Abby wanted to look away as the man's hand was removed by teeth that seemed to be as sharp as razorblades and jaws, she now knew could snap bone.

The shock of his hand being bitten off was too much. The man passed out, still bleeding, while Shiva disappeared into the brush, taking the man's hand and gun with him.

Abby looked at the other man on the camera screens. He was holding his ear, calling out, looking at the door in front of him. He slapped a box on the door and ran away. Abby saw the bright flash of light on the camera lens as it widened out, showing both the man and the door, and then she heard a big, loud noise. As the smoke cleared, the man walked to the door, gun in hand, only to find it fully intact.

The man put his hand on the door and pulled it away. Obviously it was hot. That is when Alan, very quiet for a man his size, appeared behind him and locked the man in a choke hold. The man struggled but Alan lifted him off the ground as he held him in the debilitating hold. Moments later the man went limp, and Alan let him fall to the ground.

Alan looked at the door, and Abby ran to it. She opened the door and swung the massive locks that were imbedded in the ground and foundation beams, then swung the door open to find Alan there.

"You ok?" Alan asked.

"Yeah," Abby said. "I am glad you kept one alive. The other two are probably not." She explained the last several minutes and Alan whistled three short bursts as Shiva came trotting toward him, carrying a hand with a gun still in it in his mouth. Vishnu sniffed Shiva for a moment but paid complete attention to Alan at all times.

"Well," Alan said, "looks like Shiva has shown us the type of gun used. We need to see if we can get more information out of our survivor. Maybe start cleaning up the bodies from the back of the house also, before they start attracting vultures. I mean, we are starting to stack them up down there."

Abby giggled. "Funny."

"Humor gets us through," Alan said.

"Michael thinks that too," Abby said.

"He is a funny guy sometimes," Alan said. "Michael used to make me laugh a lot. His mom thought he was the best and funniest guy ever."

Abby smiled for a moment, thinking about the strange links between Alan, Michael, and all of the things they had learned since they met this man.

Alan walked to the man in front of him and Abby. Though he weighed about 180 pounds, Alan grabbed the back of his neck and stood him up, the man's feet dragging as Alan pulled him into the house.

The two dogs paced alongside Alan until they got to the house. Alan set the man down and put his hand up in exclamation. The dogs looked eager and paid close attention to him. Alan then drew a circle in the air and the two took off following each other into the brush.

Alan grabbed the man's collar again and drug him over to a kitchen chair then looked at Abby. "Is this okay? Or we can go to my house as I have a chair for this," Alan said.

"It's fine. I doubt it will stain," Abby smiled.

Alan zip-tied the man's hands behind his back then his legs to the legs of the chair. He then ran two long zip-ties from the legs back to the hands of the man, effectively locking him in place. Even breaking the chair would not free the man, making the prison relatively secure. Alan then checked the man's pulse. "He is fine, just asleep," he stated. Then Alan took out his Swiss Army knife and worked out the earpiece from the man's ear.

"Water?" Alan said.

"Sure," Abby said, grabbing a glass from the kitchen and filling it.

Alan took the glass, drank half of it and turned to Abby. "Thanks," he said, then threw the remaining water into the man's face and watched him wake and shake his head as if trying to knock out the cobwebs stuck inside. "Low tech but works every time." Alan smiled. The man looked around the room with increasing clarity then almost panic as realization dawned on him. Alan asked the man, "What shall we talk about?" The man gritted his teeth and Alan smiled again.

Chapter 7

Just outside of Lexington, Kentucky in Richmond, is the Bluegrass Army Depot, a storage facility for a great many things no one wants to think about. It includes a variety of weapons that many people wish had never been created. The staff at this facility are well trained and always ready for anything. They also take care of the tedious process of slowly eliminating the most heinous weapons in a safe manner. It takes time, budget, and a lot of work, but they are great at what they do.

There is a small addition to the Bluegrass Army Depot that is not well know if known at all. It is a team of people, responsible for cleaning up a series of issues that were created by the government or that need to be solved by the government, with minimal oversight. The team, once banded together to find Michael Masterson, is defined by the people within it who, by their very nature, are outside the norm of other soldiers. Their very purpose is to protect the country in whatever way they can.

Alex Brown walked down the corridor in the Bluegrass Army Depot. He was heading to the mess hall to get lunch, reading a small file as he went. Most of what he read was available in electronic format, but he preferred the old-style paper because he could touch it, feel it, and of course write all over it as necessary. As Alex walked into the mess hall, he saw a table with a few people surrounding it. It had been his experience that the table would probably be where his team would be gathered. As he approached, he saw who had the crowd's attention. Jim was telling one of his many stories again, and everyone was laughing and asking him questions as he went.

"I mean, who would have thought I was walking in on a wedding?" Jim continued, and Alex smiled. He had heard this story of how Jim had been sent to take out a group of terrorists and it turned out to be a wedding. Jim went on. "I mean, I walked in with a team behind me, guns locked and loaded in standard "ooo-rah mode" when we get in the room. It was just after the priest had said, 'If anyone has just cause these two young people should not be wed, speak now or forever hold your peace.' Here we rush in looking like the damn army, which of course we were, and the groom fainted, while the mother of the bride started chasing us with her purse while I was trying to explain."

The crowd was laughing profusely as Ronnie, the youngest member of their team asked, "So what happened then?"

Jim smiled. Ronnie was always very naïve, but he was learning fast in the team Alex had put together. "Well, I talked the mother of the bride down, we all stayed for the wedding and saw the new couple get married, and I got a date with one of the bridesmaids. All in all, a good night," Jim said.

The crowd laughed again as Alex quietly went, "Uh hum."

The group looked back and saw Alex and started to disburse all over the room. All that was left was his team. Jim looked at him and started eating his eggs. "Party pooper," he said as he smiled and took a mouthful.

"Yeah, yeah," Alex said, looking at his old friend. He and Jim had been through a lot together. They were in the service for a long time across several areas, and Jim was always that wildcard who got people out in a pinch. He was a fantastic soldier, but he was also a bit of a joker. This had kept his rank low all through their service days. Alex had called him after a particularly bad time in Ivel, Kentucky. A bad time that left the rest of his crew dead. It was a whirlwind after that, and Alex recruited Jim to be part of his new team. Well, maybe not fully recruited, more like drafted.

Seated next to Jim was Ronnie Comer. Ronnie was a

Kentucky born and bred patriot. He was curious and seemed simple, but he pushed the envelope on every task he was given, simply because he would not fail. He had blamed it on his family. They thought this country was the greatest country in the world, and if you were going to enlist, it was your duty to give everything you could at every moment.

Across from Ronnie was Rachel Brown. Rachel had been recruited after sparring with Jim and proving she was driven and tenacious. Both her and Ronnie were stationed at the Depot prior to joining the team. The fact the team worked out of the Depot as a whole was due plain and simple to them all living close, and it being central to almost anywhere. Besides, who would look for a covert team whose primary jobs were extreme and violent in central Kentucky?

There were several other members of the team that were not at the table at the moment, and one had recently died. Alex was sad over her death but did not dwell on it. He had not dwelled on his long-term friend, Mark, when he had been killed by a missile attack outside of Ivel, KY. It was too easy to get lost in despair if you let it take you. You had to let it go and move on.

Alex looked over at Jim. He seemed happy now, but the death of Lisa, one of the team, had hit him hard. Alex was well aware that even though Jim was easy going and seemed untouchable, he felt things very deeply.

The newest member of the team, Melody King, walked into the mess hall and sat down next to Alex. "You asked me to look into the Masterson files and see if there were more loose ends. Well, I did what I could with the available files, but they are nearly black from redaction. Is there any way we can get originals?" Melody asked, getting straight to business.

"I will see what I can do," Alex said.

"Hi Mel," Jim said. "Want some eggs?" At that moment, Jim stuck out his tongue with a mouthful of eggs on it.

Melody looked at him. "Cute," she said in a gruff voice. "When do they put you out for recess?" she asked Jim.

"They won't let me out. I keep looking up the teacher's skirt," Jim said.

"Idiot," Melody said with a smile.

"Thanks," Jim said. "My mom told me to aspire to be good at something. Being an idiot works."

Although they bantered back and forth, Jim and Melody had a close call recently that gave them mutual respect for each other. They both mourned the death of Lisa also, whom Melody barely had known. It was part of being a team, and more than just a team, a family.

Alex looked at the group. "With the General recovering, I have asked Melody to scan the files Masterson worked on. It will give us a place to clean up while we wait for further orders. Until she comes up with something, we have some free time to work on weapons, tactics, getting the planes in shape or some R and R."

Jim smiled. "I like the last one," he said.

Alex looked at him. "I thought you would, Jim. Three days for everyone but Mel and I work?"

Rachel smiled. "Yep." She looked at Jim and asked, "Where we going?"

"What do you mean, we?" Jim asked.

"C'mon Jim. You are always talking about your legendary bar scenes. Let's go visit one and take a few days off," Rachel whined with a twinkle in her eye.

Ronnie joined in. "Yeah, I would like to see you in action," he told Jim.

Rachel looked at Ronnie., "They will be checking your ID all night. You look 12, Ronnie."

Jim laughed. "Yeah, sure, whatever. How about we go up to Belterra and just gamble and have some fun?"

"Belterra is usually pretty lame. How about we go somewhere else?" Rachel asked.

Jim looked at Rachel. "Fine," he said, then turned to Alex and asked, "Can we borrow a plane?"

Alex looked at Jim. "What?"

"May as well take them to Vegas," Jim said. "Then maybe Rachel will shut up for a while."

"Call Terry and Barbara," Alex replied. "They said they needed to run some test flights on the 650. This would be a good time to do it, and they could check it while in Vegas after a flight there. Remember it is government property and not a taxi service. If they say no, find a way on your own."

Jim smiled. "Yes, sir," he said in an almost nice tone.

Melody pulled out a file and showed it to Alex. "These are the ones I have concerns about. It would be good if we could get unredacted copies."

Alex looked at her Melody. "Yeah, like I said, I will see what I can do."

Melody looked at him. "We could all work from Vegas, and you know Jim, it might be good for us to be close. We can work from anywhere."

Alex looked at Melody and said, "Jim's a big boy. Your point?"

"Well, sir, you probably need some unwind time too," Melody said to Alex, "and I could do with a show and a drink."

"You might be right, Melody," Alex said.

"Jim," Alex said a little louder to the group and they all looked at him. "Change of plans. We are all going to Vegas. Mel and I will work from there while the rest of you yuck it up for a while. Tell Terry to put in a flight plan and have Barbara get us rooms at something cheap."

Jim laughed. "I have comps on most of the strip. Let me get us a room."

Alex shook his head and said, "Of course you do. Get us a room then, Jim. Pack up everybody, and let's get going in 4 hours. I will leave the details to you and know that it is all in good hands."

There was a wry smile on Jim's face as he searched for the words that would make everyone laugh. Instead, Jim saluted, and got up with Rachel and Ronnie. They all walked to the door and headed into the compound.

Alex looked down at the file Melody had given him. He turned but she too had walked away. He flipped through the pages. Most of them were covered with "Bastard Son," Michael's call sign, and "Termination," which made Alex wonder what was hidden deep in the past these files represented. Hopefully the clues would lead nowhere, and nothing would be necessary, no fights, no endless stakeouts, no bloodshed, no Michael. Hopefully.

Chapter 8

Alan had spent quite a while asking questions of the defiant man in front of them. Abby sat back and watched as he only got smart remarks from the man they had captured. He was not gaining ground being nice.

Alan looked at Abby. "I am the wrong person to be asking questions."

Abby looked quizzical and asked, "Really?"

"Yeah," Alan said to Abby.

Abby looked at the man. "Well, I am out of time and the clock is ticking for Michael."

"Yes, it is you little bitch!" the man spat.

Abby quickly walked over to the man, and as she reached him, drew the twelve-inch knife and imbedded it into his femur. As she did it, she felt the knife burry into the bone and knew the pain was excruciating.

"Call me a bitch again," she said, as the man rocked with the pain he was feeling. Abby then put her foot on his leg and pulled out the knife.

"Where's Michael?" she demanded.

The man said, "Fuck.." but before he could finish his response, Abby had put the knife into the femur of his other leg. The man screamed again, but this time Abby used his groin to hold his body down as she pulled out the knife. The man was in real pain when Abby repeated, "Where's Michael?"

The man did not answer right away so Abby pulled back the knife. Then he screamed, "Wait!"

Abby stopped. "Yes?" she asked.

"I don't know where he is," the man said. "I was hired a few weeks ago through my agent. I didn't know where we were going or who we were hitting until today."

"You must know something," Abby said.

The man grimaced in pain. "All I know is that we were in town at the hotel until they called us."

"How many more?" Alan asked the man.

"I don't know," the man spat. "Jesus, this hurts."

Abby looked at the man. "How do you communicate?" she asked him.

"The earpieces, damnit, the earpieces," the man said in obvious pain.

"We'll see," Abby said.

Alan pulled out a small box and turned the knob on. It was tuned to the same channel he had monitored earlier. The transmitter buzzed.

"Respond."

Abby and Alan listened while the man sat moaning. "Sir, I think everyone is down, we are moving in to investigate. Tracking says the girls phone is still inside."

Alan was up in a moment, grabbing the man's weapon and running to the door.

Abby said, "Wait!" but it was too late, as Alan swung the door open and realized the other men were closer than he had considered. The bullets seemed to fly at him in slow motion as he moved the door to close it. It was too late. A stray bullet passed through the meat of his arm and through his calf before the door could be closed. Alan then rolled to the side as three men burst into the house through the now open impervious door.

The men had forgotten one thing. Abby was there. She held up the P90. Most people don't realize the P90 can effectively shoot almost 900 rounds per minute. True, it only has a 50-round magazine, but it is highly effective in mid quarters combat. The bullpup design allowed Abby to hold the weapon close and simply spray the three overconfident men now inside of her house. The high velocity bullets did the rest, ripping apart the men in quick order.

Abby expended the 50 shots in her first magazine in only a moment as brass tinkled to the ground like metal snowflakes hitting a tin roof. Before they could even finish falling, she had pulled off the magazine and dropped another into place. One of the men started to turn over, but a short spray stopped him from moving. The other two lay still, either dead or locked in fear of the onslaught that had just been released. Her captive was panting after seeing his comrades dropped so easily.

Alan sat up and the door swung open as a fourth man pushed on it. He raised his weapon only to have it removed, as Shiva and Vishnu each grabbed an arm and pulled him to the ground. His struggles were brief as Alan moved to the door. He gave no command to pause or stop, so the dogs simply finished what they had started. Razor sharp teeth broke bone and ripped flesh.

The man quivered, then stopped, and both dogs became puppies and ran to Alan.

Abby walked toward the fourth man. She pointed the gun directly at his face. "Where is Michael?" she demanded. "I am done playing!"

"Really," the man sobbed, "I don't know." Abby tensed her finger and he said, "They said somewhere in Detroit or Michigan or something. I don't know anymore."

Abby was suddenly calm. "Thanks," she said as she moved to Alan and looked at his wounds. Turning his leg first, Abby said, "No bullet in here." Then she checked his arm. "Not one here either."

Alan smiled and made a bit of a groan. The two black German Shepherds looked at him, wagged their tails and licked his face. "Yeah, no bullets but I might drown." Alan smiled.

Abby smiled. "I need to get you to a doctor," she said.

Alan tried to get up, but his leg was not about to allow his weight on it, and he dropped back to the floor. "Hmm, that's not going to work yet," Alan said.

"Dingbat," Abby smiled. "You need to sit here and wait."

Alan reached into his pocket and pulled out what looked like two large aspirins. "Water, please?" he asked, and Abby grabbed a bottle of water from the table she had been standing at earlier. Alan poured the water over the items and they expanded quickly. He then unfolded them and Abby saw two full cloths. He used those to wrap his leg tightly. He then took out 2 more and wet those as well. Once they were full size, he used them to wrap his arm. The dressings were neat and clean, and Alan sat back against the wall.

"Neat toys. You and Michael exchange notes often?" Abby laughed. "I will get help."

"Umm, how are you going to explain a stack of bodies in the house and yard and me?" Alan asked.

Abby looked around, then thought about the perimeter. There were men everywhere lying dead in and around her house. "Good question," Abby said. "Any ideas?"

Alan laughed then cringed as it hurt to laugh. He reached into his pocket and brought out a very small cell phone. He looked at it, used one hand to scroll through numbers, then dialed. A moment later the phone was answered. Alan said, "Maid service." Then he paused and said, "Silent Wolf." Alan paused again, and in a few moments said, "GPS target." After another moment, he said, "Verified. 2 hours ETA." Alan then laid down the phone next to him and slid over near the door. "We need to get the bodies inside so no one can see. The ones out back are no issue but the ones in the front may draw suspicion if anyone comes," Alan said.

Abby nodded. The man outside the front door was a bloody mess. Alan looked at the dogs, held a finger in the air, pointed at the body and to the floor next to the others. The two dogs wagged their tails profusely and ran to the man in seconds. Then, like machines, they grabbed on to the man's shoulders and drug him inside the house. The dogs each weighed perhaps 100 pounds, and the man was an easy 230 but they had moved him like he was a cheap playtoy.

It took a few minutes, but Abby went outside and policed brass and made the front lawn look as though nothing had happened. She came back into the house and Alan was wrapped in a small silver blanket. "It was in my pocket," he said, smiling. "Adrenaline is fading. I don't want to go into shock."

Abby went to the bedroom and brought out a quilt. She knelt down and wrapped Alan in it. "It will get bloody," he said.

"No biggie. I will make another one," Abby responded.

"You are full of surprises," Alan laughed. "So now we wait," he said.

Abby looked at the man in the chair. "What about him?"

"We will take care of him when the cleaners get here," Alan said.

"Alan," Abby said. "I can't wait. I need to start chasing this down. We have the darts and the weapons that fire them. Maybe this Larry guy can help me track them down."

"Yeah, but you can't go alone..." Alan started to say.

"Watch me," Abby said. "I saved your ass, and I can damn sure save Michael's." She continued, "If I can find him."

Alan smiled. "Look, get to Grand Rapids, Michigan, and I will have Melody meet you there."

Abby smiled. "Still think I can't do it alone?"

Alan laughed and closed his eyes. "No, but I know she can find a needle in a hayfield. You might need that."

Abby smiled. "OK, but keep the rest of them out of it," she said.

Alan looked at her and told her, "No promises."

Abby ran downstairs and came up with a bag. She then scurried to her room and moments later came back with a second bag that was small in size.

"Never seen a woman pack that light," Alan laughed.

"Never been around me," Abby said. "Besides, I can buy whatever I need, except weapons."

"Grand Rapids," Alan said. "I will call Melody."

Abby picked up her cell phone and hit a button. "Jay," she said and waited. "Relocation," she said into the phone. "Got it, DBS in 60," she heard. Abby smiled.

She knelt by Alan. "Will you be ok?" she asked him.

Alan smiled. "Sure. When you get back your house will be as good as new." He nodded to her, "Leave your phone here, they are tracking it."

"How can I call," Abby started.

"Jay will have a burn I am sure, or pick one up, but you can't use the same phone," Alan said. "Don't worry, it will be here and like I said, the house will be good as new."

"Make sure you get the dog hair," Abby smiled.

Alan frowned, "I brush them all the time."

"I was kidding," Abby said as she stood. She left her phone on the kitchen table and wondered how she would get anyone. She pushed aside the thought and went on.

Abby went downstairs to the garage. She got to the Suburban and stopped, got out and looked to the other side of the garage. She went to the covered car, her baby. She uncovered the waiting beauty below, a sleek Aston Martin Db9 that was anticipating its use. Abby put her bags in the spacious trunk and got into the driver's seat. She admired the sleek finishes as much as the first day she saw the car. She had seen it in Paris at a dealership downtown and had fallen in love with it. Michael had gotten it for her a few months before, and she had not driven it more than 1,000 miles. The sleek black car was an amazing piece of engineering and would be far faster than the Suburban. She might stick out a little, but it would be worth it.

Abby started the car and heard the predatory roar of the engine. She backed out of the garage and hit "close" on her remote and watched the garage seal. Abby then headed down the driveway to the airport.

Chapter 9

Melody's phone rang as she was going over files in the plane, on her way to Vegas with the group. Alex looked up, but Melody smiled when she saw the number and went to the back of the plane. "Hey sexy," she said. "Feel like flying down to Vegas?" Melody listened and went to the back of the plane. "What?" She asked. "I see." She said quietly. "Yes, I can help as soon as I know you are ok," she said quietly. "No, your dogs can't fix a bullet wound." "Ok." Melody said in response to some statement. "I love you too."

Melody sat down in the seat at the back of the cabin. She looked like she was pondering some long-lost issue that no one else had ever discovered. Her long black hair draped around her face. To most men she would look like a goddess. At the moment, she was tearing up a little but gained her composure and walked back to the front of the cabin.

Alex looked at her. "You ok?"

"I'm fine," Melody said. "I have work to do."

Alex looked at her again, then across the seats at Jim. Jim shrugged at him. "Don't ask me," he said.

Melody stared at her computer screen while being perplexed by the call she just had. Alan had been shot, Abby was on her way to Michigan, and Michael had been kidnapped. Alan had asked her to keep it quiet if she could, but she considered that maybe it would not be good to keep this one a secret.

"Alex," Melody started, "we may have a problem, but I need you to hear me out before you start barking orders."

"Okay," Alex said as Jim leaned forward.

"You too," Melody said to Jim.

Jim smiled and said, "Sure, whatever."

"Alan has been shot," Melody said. "He didn't tell me much, but Abby is chasing whoever took Michael. Alan said he will be okay, but who knows how this will work?"

"Where is Abby going?" Alex asked, "and Michael has been taken?"

"Alan didn't tell me much, but he said I should meet Abby,' Melody said. "I told him I was on my way to Vegas and he said he would have her meet me there. He also said not to tell you."

Alex smiled. "Still has trust issues, even after DC."

Melody smiled back weakly. "Of course he does. He has a lot of issues with the government, and you should know why."

Alex frowned for a moment. "Okay, Mel, what's our play?" he asked.

Melody looked at Alex sideways for asking for an opinion. "Well, let's land in Vegas and figure it out. I will meet Abby and we can decide how to proceed from there."

Alex looked at the floor. "Okay, we will play it cool for now, but if Masterson is captured, we know that might not be good."

Jim looked at Alex with seriousness. "I just want to see who caught him unaware."

Alex looked at the floor. "Yeah, me too."

Chapter 10

The Happy Scotsman was a plane that virtually anyone would recognize. The fat C130J Hercules had a massive Scotsman in a kilt painted on the side, and wherever it went it drew a crowd. This would be the third time it landed in Dubois. Jay guided the plane down expertly on a runway not necessarily big enough for the hulking aircraft. The good part was that he was not argued with since this wasn't the first time he had been there. Instead, the tower simply cleared him, and he landed. Much easier than all that foreplay he had before.

As the plane came to a halt, Jay opened the back and walked out on the ramp, spying the Black DB9 that now drove straight to him. He was surprised to see Abby get out of the car and yell, "Howdy, Jay!"

"Hey, Abby," Jay said. "Where's Michael?"

Abby frowned. "That's what we need to solve. Can I bring her on board?"

Jay looked at her and motioned her in. The ramps allowed the DB9 or much bigger vehicles to actually load into the plane and be off anywhere they needed to go. Jay must have been close for him to get here in an hour so that would be her first question.

"Jay, were you here for something?" Abby asked.

"No, I was heading back to Kentucky from Seattle. Was already up and you were right on the way," Jay said. "What is this about Michael? Where is he?"

Abby frowned again. "He was taken, shot with a dart gun then taken somewhere. The only real clues we have are somewhere in Michigan, and a gun that Alan thinks could be traced by a guy outside of Grand Rapids."

"You call Alex and his group?" Jay asked.

"Alan called Melody, and I need to call him. Do you have a phone I can use, mine was being tracked," Abby asked.

"Melody?" Jay asked.

"A new person in the team," Abby said. "She was brought on to help track a weird case. She is good, and well, as it sometimes goes, she and Alan met and they had instant chemistry, so they hooked up. Well, it has been fireworks ever since."

Jay laughed one of his big belly laughs. "It is always something. I miss the scariest things, don't I?"

Jay handed Abby his cell phone and she dialed a number quickly. Jay raised his eyebrows.

"What," Abby said.

"Most people don't know numbers anymore, they trust their phones," Jay said with a grin.

"Yeah," she said, "It is an easy number."

Abby paused and then said, "Well?" to the phone.

There was another pause, "I don't like it, but we will head there."

Jay laughed as Abby hung up, "Where to?"

"Vegas," Abby said. "It appears Melody will be there."

Jay smiled and looked out the back door.

Abby smiled. "Jay, you look like you have lost weight."

Jay laughed again. "Yeah, Janet is trying to work it all off me," he said.

"I bet," Abby said. "Sounds like fun."

Jay laughed again, and Abby realized she missed his jovial attitude. To Jay, there was always a joke, usually about a bar. If not a joke, he had stories of bars for days, as it seems he had been to every bar on the planet.

"Any reason to stay?" Jay asked.

"No, I am ready," Abby said. "Any issue if we change the flight plan to Vegas?" she asked.

"No issue," Jay said. "I will call it in as we start up. You still remember how to fly this thing?" he asked Abby.

"Where is Janet?" Abby asked.

"Janet is with her friends at a spa in French Lick, Indiana. Of course, I have to work. I would have liked to have had some people massaging my damn back for a few days." Jay laughed.

"All day job, Jay," Abby said as the back of the plane closed up. She and Jay walked to the cockpit and Abby settled into the copilot chair.

"GYZa55 Heavy request clearance for takeoff," Jay said into the headset as he settled into the big pilot's chair. Abby had already begun spinning up engines as he busied himself with the preflight checklist that he had not finished.

"GYZa55 Heavy, request granted, cameras are rolling," the tower said.

"Roger, tower," Jay laughed. He had been all over YouTube flying this plane in and out of this little airport. It was time to run it again, and Jay lined up the nose, braked hard, ran up the engines as high as he dared, and let off the brakes. The big plane rocketed down the runway, and at the last moment, lifted from the ground, defying the odds once again.

"GYZa55, another successful video," the tower called.

"Tower, this is the Happy Scotsman. You just want me to crash someday, don't you?" Jay said into the mic.

"Gyza55, it would get us viral up here. We are getting close to a million hits on your last takeoff," the tower said.

"Tower, that it would," Jay laughed as he swung the nose of the plane towards Vegas. He turned to Abby then. "Well, you have a story to tell, lassie. Let's hear it."

Abby smiled at his patient way. She had always liked Jay. She started explaining this very hectic day to him as the plane headed to the gambling capital of the west coast.

Chapter 11

Michael was aware again. He knew he dare not make any noise or movement as it would get him injected again. So as before, he stayed loose and listened. The vehicle was stopped, and he believed that he was in the same van, potentially with the same people. He heard talking and some arguing outside. Michael struggled to listen.

"What the fuck do you mean, she killed them all?" a voice was demanding. "I paid good money for your handpicked team, and they fell to a woman?"

Michael wanted to smile. They had not gotten Abby yet, and she apparently was making a mess out of their plans. He continued to listen.

"Who?" the voice was quivering with anger. "That's supposed to make it okay? One man, a girl and a few dogs take out a full team? You people are morons!"

Michael struggled to try to place the voice, but he did not recognize it. If this person was paying for the team, he had some type of vested interest in the operation.

Michael thought about how he had opened the window to let the breeze in to the house. It was something he did often, but not when he was in the shower. He soon regretted doing so. When he had come out, a masked gunman was there. As fast as Michael dove, he was still hit by several small darts. He had only moments, before the drugs took effect, to focus on the second man coming in the window. He remembers thinking how the team did not seem very well organized. They were not covering each other and instead just looking for him. He thought that they knew of him, but maybe were not truly aware of his past or his skills. Perhaps that would give Michael an advantage.

The voice got loud again. "Yes, we will be on a plane to Detroit as soon as possible. We drove to Jackson Hole's Airport, and as the name says, it is a hole."

Michael thought about Detroit. He considered the people he knew in Michigan and who might have a grudge against him or Abby. As he was thinking about that, he also thought of the love of his life and hoped she was okay. With Alan there, Abby would have more than a fighting chance, depending on the number of people this guy had hired.

"Yeah, I swear he is out. I will keep him on ice till we get there. No, the drug won't kill him. Hell, he woke up from it once and it should have kept him down for 8 hours. We will keep an eye on him though. I still don't get your..." The voice stopped, and Michael strained, thinking something else was going on.

"Yes, sir, I know it is none of my business. Yes, I know, yes, sir, I know. Thank you, sir, goodbye," the voice said.

Michael heard the man stomp around. He was sure that was two separate people. One a subcontractor, and the man talking on this end of the phone a subcontractor as well. He thought that was interesting. Maybe the man knew Michael through an agent.

"Yeah, bring the plane up," Michael heard the voice talking again. "I want to make sure we are in the air quickly. The sooner we are rid of this package the better."

Michael opened his eyes a crack and saw that the back of the van was empty, and the doors were closed. He strained to see in the reflection anything behind him, but he could not. He would have to once again take a chance on looking back. He did, and the man sitting there was not paying any attention this time. Michael slowed his breathing and waited.

The side door slid open. "He awake yet?" a man asked.

"No," the man behind him said. "Not moved a muscle."

"Good, cover him up," the man said.

For the first time since he became aware of himself in the van, Michael realized he was naked.

"If he wakes up, get some shorts on him, or get some shorts on him while he is asleep. I don't care, but cover him up," the man said.

The man behind him laughed. "Sure, right."

Inside, Michael laughed.

Chapter 12

The G650 glided down to the runway like a feather slowly falling from the sky. The amazingly engineered aircraft was guided down by Terry and Barbara who were both skilled pilots. When the wheels touched the tarmac, there was a sensation of suddenly being on the road, and Alex liked it that way.

Jim was laughing the moment they touched down and said, "At least we can play some slots in the airport."

Ronnie smiled. "How do you play?" he asked innocently.

Jim laughed. "Living that close to casinos and you have never been?"

Ronnie looked perplexed. "I was always taught it was a fool's errand to gamble, and that the house always took the money of those who spent it on that wasteful endeavor."

Jim laughed. "Ronnie, endeavor is an awfully big word for you."

Rachel broke in. "Don't listen to him, Ronnie. That's one of the smartest things I have ever heard you say."

Ronnie smiled a little from being praised by Rachel. It was not often that she did anything but pick at him. It had been that way all the time when they were at the Depot together. Rachel was more of a bully then. When Alex and Jim had come, Rachel had started changing. She was still tough, but she knew she could be beaten easily, just not as easily as anyone else. Jim sure showed her one back then when she pushed him to spar. Ronnie remembered that he thought he was crazy for fighting her, but Jim was something called a Grandmaster, and that made him a really good fighter.

Jim laughed. "You are right, Ronnie. It is a good idea not to gamble. Then again, I think we gamble with our lives every day we work for Tarkington, so why not?"

Ronnie shrugged. Rachel laughed, and Alex was smiling a little. Melody, on the other hand, was chomping at the bit and picked up her phone and once again dialed Alan. It obviously rang several times and then went to voicemail.

Alex put his hand on Melody's arm. "He will be okay. You have read his file. Alan has been through a lot before and always lived through it."

Melody looked down. "I know, and I know he is older than me too. He pushes too hard."

Jim laughed, and Melody shot him a glare. Jim put up his hands in a mock surrender. "Sorry Mel, I just wanted to add, 'that's what she said,' but I knew it might be wrong, so I didn't."

Melody looked at Jim. "You know, it goes back and forth on whether I like you or hate you," she said.

Jim smiled. "Just don't tell the Mountain. He would probably sic his dogs on me."

Melody glared at Jim again, and Rachel looked at him too. "Shit,' she said. "From what I hear, I really wouldn't wanna' risk that, Jim."

"Yeah, I talked to one of the agents Tarkington sent to get Abby in that San Antonio gig. He said the damn thing about broke his arm," Jim said.

The plane taxied to a halt and the group got up and started grabbing their luggage. Alex stopped them. "Leave it," he said. "We will decide if we need to bug out after Abby lands. If we have to go, we don't need to repack. With cell phones on, you can go into town, but be ready to get here on the double."

"Alex," Melody said, "I am going to stay here to work and keep trying Alan."

"I am staying as well," Alex said.

Ronnie looked at the two of them and said, "I will stay too."

Barbara came out of the cockpit and looked at Ronnie. "No, you are not. We are going to go for a walk."

Ronnie looked at Barbara in her sharp khaki pants and black shirt, with her hazel eyes and blazing red hair, and simply said, "Yes, ma'am." As he began to walk out of the plane, Barbara looked back at Alex and winked. Alex knew she liked Ronnie, but he also knew that she had just gotten him off the plane so Alex could work. It was a nice gesture and maybe it would do them both good.

The plane was empty except for Melody and Alex. "Melody, look," Alex said. "There's a lot going on and I am sure Alan is okay. You have to remember though, Michael and the people he has been around are pretty dangerous. You need to prepare for the worst."

As if on cue, Melody's phone rang. She looked at the number and it was not recognized. She slid the icon anyway and answered, "Hello?"

"Hi," came Alan's voice. "Sorry for the delay. I have been a little engaged."

Melody took a deep breath. "You scared me, but you sound better. Where are you?" she asked Alan.

"I am still at Michael's. The cleaners have gone, and they even patched me up pretty good. Fifty-five stiches, antibiotics, and a tetanus shot. I will live. No bullets, and just a few new scars. My stupidity for opening the door." Alan said.

"Can I put you on speaker?" Melody asked.

"Alex, I guess?" Alan said, "Sure."

The phone got loud, and Alex spoke first. "So, what happened to you?"

"Easy," Alan started. "I thought I had more time and opened the door to a flurry of bullets. I got shot in the bicep and in the calf, but I will be okay, no issue."

"I mean what happened as a whole, not just to you." Alex said.

"Well, Abby called and said she had an assailant in the house," Alan replied. She had disarmed him and determined he climbed up through a window. I ran over here with the dogs, and we tried to question the first guy, who promptly threw himself out of Michael's back window. A nice 200-foot drop." Alan went on. "Once we started checking him out, I found a transmitter in his ear. It was a pretty good earbud that was deep, so someone was monitoring him, us, and pulling all the strings. The guy was starting to cooperate when he jumped, so there must have been something weird being said."

Alex laughed. "Must have been."

"So, anyway," Alan continued, "I ran home and checked the transmitter, got the frequency, pulled out a mini monitor, and then ran back to Michael's house when I heard that company was coming for Abby. She locked down the house and we got there in time to mop up. Problem was that constituted wave one, and when I went out to catch the second wave, they caught me."

"So, how did you get out of it?" Alex asked.

"Well, they didn't think Abby was a combatant. She had that damn P90 loaded down and dropped 2 magazines into them. What was left was ripped in half by Shiva and Vishnu," Alan said.

Alex asked one more question. "So, how far is it to your house?"

"About 6 miles, and yes, I got my steps in for the day." Alan laughed.

Melody broke in. "I am glad you are okay."

Alan started talking again. "Anyway, they took Michael with some mini dart, and we have no idea where. Best we can figure, he was coming out of the shower when they nailed him. The darts are small, and I don't know what they are using for a sedative, but it must've been quick."

"Why?" Alex asked.

"You have never been in Michael's house. There are weapons all over the place, hidden in secret books, boxes, cabinets, dishes. Hell, I saw one built into the frame of his toilet. If he had a second, they would have been dead," Alan said.

Alex laughed a little. "Okay, I get it. So, where is Abby?"

Alan paused. "Apparently Jay was in the area. She is probably airborne by now, heading to Vegas to get Melody. I told her I would not talk to you, so I need you to stay in the background. She will not be happy if she thinks I interfered, and she can disappear pretty quickly as well."

Alex considered for a moment. "Okay, so we can shadow, and Melody can keep us up to date, or try to convince Abby to bring us in," he said.

Alan laughed. "Good luck with that. She still thinks you are a puppet of her father, even after their recent, more pleasant reunion."

Alex thought for a second. "Well, we will try and go from there," he said.

Melody opened up again and asked, "So, how are you getting home?"

Alan was laughing. "On dog slobber, I think. Actually, they have a quad here. I will just ride it home. No issues and no six-mile walk."

Melody smiled. "Are they okay?" she asked about the dogs.

Alan laughed. "They will need a bath. They are okay though. I will let them swim in the pool for a while to get the blood off them," he said.

Melody smiled and said softly, "I am glad they are okay, and I am glad you are okay too."

There was a moment of silence. "Seems like forever since I have seen you, but it has only been a week," Alan said to Melody.

Melody smiled and looked at Alex. He nodded. "I think we will get to see you soon. For now, you stay home, and we will take care of this."

Alan laughed. "You are kidding, right?" he said.

Melody was a little sterner. "Alan, we have this. Let us work on it and you stay home. You have done enough."

Alex broke in. "Alan, can you see if you can find anyone who would be interested in Michael, or who has been looking around lately?"

Alan laughed. "That list would be long, Alex," he stated.

Alex continued. "Maybe it will give us a start. Let Abby and Melody play out the lead and we will see where ours goes. They can't just drive him to wherever. We need to start looking for airports that a van or truck or trailer or something was used with a private plane. We will send out a notice to all the air traffic controllers to keep an eye out, and push for the ground control groups as well. Maybe get a list of all private planes that have taken off in the past 2 hours up to 2 hours from now. If it were you, where would you go?" he asked Alan.

Alan paused on the other end of the phone. "Maybe Jackson, maybe even Salt Lake. Long drives, but it would be harder to guess at one. The nice part is Dubois is off the beaten path. Not many real airports around, but there are lots of scrub fields that would work, if necessary."

"Anyway, we can look for those as well," Alex said.

"I will run a script and start looking," Alan said. "I will get to my house and log on to a server and get this rolling."

"Thanks, Alan. I know you don't owe us anything, but we are looking for the same person," Alex said.

"Yeah, I know," said Alan. "Can I talk to Melody for a moment in private?"

Melody picked up the phone, nodded several times, then simply said, "I know, I love you too."

Alex walked outside of the plane for a minute. He looked at the sky and saw clouds far away. They were dark and foreboding, like a storm was getting ready to come. He saw the lightning flash in the distance.

Alex then thought about the last year with his new team and considered all the things they had gone through, another storm. He was starting to get used to the storms, and that could be a bad thing. Alex would get find the source of this kidnapping and then the storm would come.

Chapter 13

Jay was serious. "Abby, why don't you let me go after Michael? I mean, he would kill me if he knew I let you do this."

"That's sweet, Jay, but I really think I need to do this, and I don't want the cavalry involved. I appreciate your help and I will definitely have you close, but I can work through this on my own," Abby said.

"But Abby, this isn't one of yours and Michael's games. This is a real firefight with a lot of possible endpoints that just won't be good. If you die..." Jay started.

"Then I will die looking for Michael," Abby said. "There really is no debate. Michael would do the same for me, no matter what."

Jay shook his head. "You are, of course, right. I remember Michael was talking about you once in a bar in London. We had this really fine Scotch, which was supposed to be a cheap brand, but it was crisp yet smooth. The owner sold us the bottle for a dollar because he said it was awful. Anyway, Michael once said he would move the world for you if you asked. He said that he always thought of you as a friend, but when you got to know each other better, there was no one in the world that would get him like you did. I mean, how does anyone keep up with him, anyway? You find a way, and I think you keep him calmer," Jay said.

"Michael keeps Michael calmer," Abby said.

Jay laughed his belly roar. "That is like the ultimate oxymoron. When is Michael ever calm?"

Abby looked concerned. "Well, not right now. He is probably being tortured or treated badly as we speak, and there isn't anything I can do about it until I find him." Abby started to tear up, then stopped herself. "I swear, if I find these people, they will be terrified and beg me for mercy."

Jay looked at her. "Yeah, and I wouldn't want to be them if either you or Michael get ahold of them. Might be a bad day, in the essence of the word."

Abby was stoic again. The moment had passed. "So why was Michael in London?" she asked Jay.

"Why was Michael ever anywhere away from you?" Jay replied. "It was usually for your dad." He reached into a lunchbox and pulled out a bottle of water, looked at it and said, "Boy, I wish this was scotch. That time though we were over there for a private citizen. You see, Michael would sometimes take a job that was not government related to make a little more money. He was sought after by a lot of people who just needed things solved. In London, there was this Serb. He had been kidnapping little girls and selling them off to Chinese slave traders. The Bobbies could prove nothing, so the guy kept walking. This guy's daughter got nabbed and they somehow found a way to contact Michael. Well, Michael went in, and with his typical charming personality, persuaded a few guys to give it up on the Serb, and then eliminated 48 people involved in the ring. In the process, he got the guy's daughter back, but she was pretty messed up."

"How so?" Abby asked.

Jay sighed. "Well, I am not sure it is good plane talk, but when they got these girls, they would string them out on heroin so they wouldn't fight as much. This girl was a mess, and the guy, some Lord, pretty much went crazy afterwards trying to get her clean. Michael got paid well, but he donated half the money to some drug foundation to help the girl. The father took care of the girl constantly and a lot of his cash went away. Michael followed up with him a few years later and the guy had gotten the girl back together, and then gotten himself back to where he needed to be."

Abby looked serious still. "Michael never told me about any of this."

Jay smiled and said, "It was one of those things that bothered him. He said in the bar if he could have only been a few days earlier, he could have saved the girl from the pain she went through. Michael never took responsibility for people like that, but he sure did that time."

Abby laughed. "What about Madison?"

Jay smiled again. "Well, Michael said he was going to throw her out, but you said to help her," he said.

Abby laughed again. "He was right, I mean, she was our friend. Why would we just put her out in the cold?"

Jay looked stern this time. "Because it was the right thing to do. Michael has done some good things and some really bad things. No matter how you slice the watermelon, whatever his good things were, most people would think they are bad as well. It just doesn't work in most people's heads how the world really works."

"What do you mean?" Abby asked.

"Easy," Jay started, "Michael will tell you too. Watch the news. We worry about the convenience store clerk who just got shot in a robbery, but not the 55 people who were shot in a quarry, never found or heard from again. We think that a massacre is 15 people in a mall or theater, but there are hundreds of murders being committed that never become a case, they just disappear. Overseas the number is higher. Why? No one cares."

"Paranoid much?" Abby asked.

"Convinced," Jay answered. "I get tired of what I have seen. If Michael was a normal man, he would be a mess. Somehow, he handles the stress, the strain, and the emotions better than anyone I have ever seen though. I mean, he should be a poster child for PTSD," Jay said, then sipped his water.

In front of them, the clouds lit up in the distance. There was a storm and they had to go through it to get to Vegas. "No issue with the storm?" Abby asked.

Jay laughed. "You know better. This thing can take a hit from a bomb and keep flying. It may get bumpy, but we are fine. Why don't you check the straps on your car while I take us up a little higher?"

Abby went out to the car and checked it over. The straps were tight on the wheels. She liked the car. She liked the car a lot. It reminded her of Michael. It was strong and powerful on the outside and the inside, but if you got into it, it was comfortable and built to take care of the people in it.

"Abby!" Jay yelled. "Better come strap in!" Abby went back to the cockpit, put on her headset and strapped herself into the copilot's chair. The rain was already hitting the windows and she knew this was going to be a long flight. She was comforted though, by knowing that she would go through the worst storm ever to get to Michael and would overcome it.

Chapter 14

Tarkington hated being idle. He was not a "sit behind a desk" type of General. He was a "fired up I will change the world one battle at a time" General. He had been told more than once that he did not fit the mold. His language and actions were not like most enlisted men had seen or would see. Generals were of a higher caliber, men that commander respect. "Poppycock", Tarkington thought and then laughed out loud for even thinking the word.

He sat in his room, considering what he wanted to do. The last several months he had been relearning how to walk and had a reasonable gate now. The damage done to his spine by the beatings he took was considerable, but he was thankful for the people who saved him, even though he would not readily admit it.

The General stood slowly, his legs able to hold him but the nerves not able to translate as well as they should. He was fighting every moment of the day because that is who he was, and he would not let anything slow him down. He would not give the bitch he put in Gitmo the satisfaction of knowing she could affect his life at all, either. He might struggle, but he would never give up, which is what that bitch wanted more than anything.

Sarah Collin's walked into the General's bedroom with a few papers in her hand. He turned and looked at her. "What the fuck! What if I had been naked?" he asked.

"I don't do miniatures, sir," Sarah shot back. Smiling, she said, "Nice to see you walking again, General. You are getting better every day. I know you are off, but I wanted to keep you up to date on a few items coming around. Seems we have a few problems in the Middle East, specifically in Iran."

"What the fuck else is new? Those fucking idiots can't cap that place down. They really need to just glass the whole country and start over," Tarkington stated dryly.

"I am sure we can take that before the Senate, and they might even pass it," Sarah said back to the General. "Or maybe not."

"Do I pay you to be such a smartass?" the General asked as he looked at Sarah.

"No, sir, you pay me to make sure you are the best you can be," Sarah responded to the General.

Tarkington looked into a mirror on the wall. His age was catching up with him. He was fit but seeing himself was almost painful. The lines of hundreds of battles were etched into his very soul, and he felt each one. Dressed in his gym shorts and a t-shirt, he thought he looked like a classic old man picture. He was just missing the suspenders and stupid socks with garters. "Yeah, he said turning to Sarah. You have done a crappy job. I look like a poorly dug Kuwait battle shithole."

"Yes, sir, you do," Sarah said grinning. "Not my fault though. You should lay off the cheeseburgers."

"Fuck you. I can never get enough cheeseburgers, and I only get one fucking burger a week anyway," Tarkington laughed back to Sarah.

"Yes, sir," Sarah smiled. "By the way, General, your team is in Vegas, and I just got a call from Alex. Something is going on with Masterson again. He stated he would update me as soon as he got details," she said.

"Little fucker," Tarkington mumbled. "I bet Masterson thinks he is special for saving my ass. If it were not for my daughter, I bet he wouldn't have come. The little shit."

"I will handle it then, sir," Sarah said to the General.

"No," Tarkington said, "I want to know what is up with them, at least. Have you heard from Abby?" he asked.

"No, sir," Sarah answered. "You know I doubt she will call unless it is pretty bad. She's very self-sufficient."

"Yeah, yeah," General Sam Tarkington said. "Must take after me, not her deadbeat mother."

"Yes, sir," Sarah said. "I suggest you walk out to the living area in case I get updates. You can walk the treadmill for a while."

"Do I look like a fucking hamster?" Tarkington snapped at Sarah.

"No, sir," Sarah replied, "but I would hate to think you would let anything slow you down. We both know you want to send another picture to hang on your girlfriend's cell wall."

"Fuck yeah!" Tarkington said. "I think this time we should go hiking and I should moon the camera. I would get a kick out of knowing that the little bitch is staring at my ass inside there."

"You want me to set that up?" Sarah asked the General.

"Do you think she likes the one of me on the beach with those five gals?" Tarkington asked. "Take a second and call the Colonel down there. Make sure it is still up facing her all the time."

"I will do that," Sarah answered Tarkington.

"Anything else?" the General asked Sarah.

"Yes, sir," Sarah said to the General. "The House committee, researching the president, wants to talk to you about your role in the president's election and his knowledge of your operation."

"Of course they do," the General said." Invite the key staff here for the interview. Tell them it will be closed door and no reporters or recordings," he ordered Sarah.

"No colorful notations?" Sarah asked Tarkington.

"They don't deserve the effort," the General told Sarah.

"Oh, and your ex-wife called," Sarah informed the General. "I told her you were still unavailable, then she whined about the detail that checked on her another time. I told her it would not happen again," she said.

"Why couldn't that stupid bitch have killed my ex-wife? I would have given her a medal instead of putting her in Gitmo!" Tarkington stated. "Tell my fucking ex that she is a fucking idiot, and that I didn't have her checked on, that a stupid goofball thought they could get to me through her but ran screaming when they saw her fucking face!" Tarkington said angrily.

"I will summarize that for her," Sarah laughed.

"You do that," Tarkington said. "Sarah..." His voice trailed off.

"Sir," Sarah said.

"Thank you," Tarkington said to Sarah with an air of concern not normally shown by the man.

"Thank you for being nice," Sarah said back to Tarkington.

"Don't let it go to your fucking head, damnit! I just mean I am glad you didn't ask for a fucking raise," Tarkington barked at Sarah.

"No, sir," Sarah said, "I am sure you would have told me to shove a jack up my ass."

"Damn right I would have! Now carry on. I have to get ready for some hiking," Tarkington told Sarah.

As he walked back and forth, Sarah slid out of his room. Alone again, Sam Tarkington limped to the bed and sat down. The sweat was beaded on his forehead from the strain of standing and talking for so long. He sat and rubbed his legs and wiped his brow. Then, with a grimace of anger and pain, he got up and started walking again.

Chapter 15

The storm pounded the Happy Scotsman, but it had been through far worse. Jay was laughing as he steered through the high winds and tried to keep the plane at least in a relatively straight line.

Abby, who had grown up and been in combat situations in planes, laughed along with Jay. They sang bad songs as the plane rumbled with the sound of angry thunder slapping the craft like a wet sponge. "41 bottles of scotch on the wall, 41 bottles of scotch," Jay started the next chorus.

The wind seemed to be trying to drive the plane somewhere, it just didn't know where, and the wipers were swinging on the windows with little effect. Jay had laughed and said, "Don't even know why I have the wipers on." The rain was so hard it was a complete whiteout before them.

As Jay and Abby sang yet another verse, the rain slowed, and the plane's speed seemed to decrease and be under control a little more. Then the skies began to clear in front of them. Looking to the rear, Jay saw the massive cloudbank that seemed to be a wall between Vegas and the world. Storms were rare in this area, but they did happen, and Jay smiled and said, "Well, I guess that was a bit of fun."

Abby looked at Jay. "As much fun as you can have in a Hercules," she said.

"She is a fine bird," Jay told Abby.

"So, you tell me," Abby said back to Jay dryly.

"Ouch," Jay said to Abby. "The Happy Scotsman is the most fun toy in the air. Make no mistake, there is nothing better."

Abby laughed. "She is a good plane," she agreed with Jay.

"We are coming into Vegas," Jay said. "Let's run the checks after that beating, Abby." "Las Vegas Tower, GYZa55 heavy requesting landing instructions," Jay keyed his mic.

"GYZa55 heavy proceed 270 and hold, you have three ahead of you," the tower returned.

Abby was busy checking items then looked at Jay. "We have an engine running hot, but it's not bad. Nothing else is showing up. Will check flaps and gear as we drop," she stated.

"Great," Jay said. "She will hold together. She has taken near hits from flak cannons and a severe beating from other anti-air fire. She can handle it," he told Abby.

"GYZa55 Heavy, clear for landing on 26r, wind 5.0 gusts to 20," the tower said on the headphones.

Jay swung around to 26r and lined up and saw a rather fat 747 touch down before him. As he slowed the plane and moved flaps out, the aircraft seemed to hang in the air. He gave it a little more and it began gliding forward again. As they approached the ground, they dropped the gear and Jay eased up slightly, adding a little more flap so the plane simply floated in. Abby was impressed with the trick, and enjoyed it when Jay would land like a commercial pilot with the beast they were in.

"Nice landing," Abby told Jay.

Jay smiled. "She is a good girl," he told Abby.

"Las Vegas ground control request parking instructions," Jay said on the mic.

"GYZa55 Heavy, proceed hanger 15B," the voice came.

"Never been there. Pull the map and look it up," Jay said to Abby.

"You know I may need a way out of this," Abby told Jay.

"I will take care of it," Jay assured Abby, "there is a burn phone over the bed. Make sure you get it."

Jay asked the tower and was given tight directions while Abby looked up the hanger and got the burn phone. "It is not on the maps," Abby said.

"Well crap," Jay said. "Probably your buddy or daddy trying to make sure we go where we are supposed to go," he said to Abby.

"Probably," Abby responded to Jay. "It will be fine."

As they approached the big hanger, Jay and Abby saw the little G650 sitting inside. As Abby expected, as they approached, Alex and Melody got out of the plane and waited for them while they parked, and the engine spun down. A ground crew ran up and chocked the wheels.

As Jay opened the back and walked out, Melody yelled to him, "You may have a problem here."

Jay walked out on the tarmac, and as he looked at the gear assembly, he saw the hydraulic fluid spraying out of a fitting. "Well damn," Jay said as he went up and locked the gear in place."

Abby walked out and asked Jay, "Bad?"

"I can fix it, but it will be a few hours, parts are on the plane," Jay said.

Alex broke in. "We have a mechanic too, I can call."

"No, not a big deal. I will get to work," Jay said as he walked back to the ramp. "Abby, fill them in," he said as he started pulling out boxes of tools.

Abby sighed. "I guess we need to catch up. Where do I start?"

Alex looked at Abby. "At the beginning, of course," he said. "You need to take a moment and think it through. Let's go to the 650. We have a table outside. We can talk it through and decide what we want to do." They walked to a large table set up in the hanger. Comfortable chairs were around it and they all sat down. "So, Abby, what is going on with Michael and how do we work together to find him and solve your problem," Alex asked.

"My problem?" Abby asked. "My problem is I'm missing Michael."

Alex tried to recover. "I know, I'm sorry," he told Abby. "Can you tell me what happened at least?"

Abby was indignant now. "How about I deal with this myself?" she said to Alex.

Alex smiled and asked Abby, "Don't you think you could use some help?"

Abby cut him off. "I can use some help. Alan sent me here for help from Melody. I don't need your team all over the place getting in the way. I know Michael has some respect for you, but I am not Michael. I have things to do and Michael to save! I don't need my father's elite team in the middle of my business telling "daddy" what is going on."

Alex sat back in the chair and looked around the hanger. "Look Abby, I want Michael to be saved as well. This isn't about the General."

"Like hell you do," Abby said to Alex.

Melody spoke up. "Abby, I will help, but I thought maybe we needed a few more people to make things work better. Can they try to help at least?"

Abby slumped in the chair. She looked up at the girders in the hanger, then over at the G650. Then she looked at Alex, wearing his jeans and black army issued t-shirt. She set her jaw as she looked at him. "You really want to help?"

"Yes Abby," Alex said.

"You sure?" Abby retorted quickly to Alex.

"Yes," Alex repeated to Abby.

"Let Melody and I take the G650. You follow when Jay finishes the Scotsman," Abby told Alex.

"Who will pilot?" Alex asked Abby. "It is a government plane."

"Don't play stupid. I think you know I can fly it, and you know Melody is qualified for a smaller plane, but she is allowed to copilot," Abby said.

"Hmm," Alex said, looking Abby over. "We never have really talked or done much together."

"Just DC," said Abby, "and you were trying to be in charge."

Alex tried to contain himself. "I was in charge," he told Abby.

Abby smiled. "You know, there is one thing I have learned in all my time with Michael. The people who always think they are in charge are allowed to think that by the ones who are really in charge. The truth always seems to be, the only thing anyone can know for sure, is that control is an illusion."

Alex bristled. "Sounds like you have been around Michael a lot, Abby," he said.

Abby chuckled. "Sounds like it, because I have. You have a decision to make, sir," she said to Alex. "I threw an offer on the table, and if you are truly wanting to help, let me head out and try to get ahead of this now. You can think about what else is going on and talk about all the details you want. I will deal with the realities of figuring some things out. Besides, we may have an advantage if we do this quickly."

Alex pondered. "Okay, Abby, deal, but only if I get all the details before you go. Also, anything else I can to learn which direction I should be looking at this from. We will need to unload our gear from the plane and get the team back."

"No," Abby told Alex.

"What?' Alex asked Abby in disbelief.

"Melody and I will go, but maybe we will do this a bit differently," Abby said to Alex.

"What do you mean?" Alex asked Abby, a little confused. Melody looked on, wondering what was happening as well.

"You know my father," Abby said. "I don't have a lot of trust in you, your team or much connected to him, but I am trying," she told Alex.

"Of course," Alex said, "but we are here to help."

"I see you are trying," Abby said, "and I wanted to believe, with Mel and Alan and all, but I wasn't sure. So, let's do this a little differently. Melody and I will take the Happy Scotsman and you will follow tomorrow. Or if you or Alan find something that helps, we will have eyes on ground with a little to spare. We will be able to go a few places without knocking down the walls of Jericho in the process."

"The plane is broken," Alex told Abby.

"That plane is perfect. It's made for deception. It was never broken. It was just a diversion, so I could find out where you really stood," Abby told Alex.

Alex shook his head, and Melody looked over to the Happy Scotsman where Jay was smiling and wiping his hands with a grimy rag. "I suppose I should expect that. I never seem to know which way is up with you, with Michael, or with the General," Alex said.

Abby nodded. "With dear old dad, I am not sure he knows which side is up often, but with me, well, this is different."

Melody, Alex, and Abby leaned forward in their chairs. Abby began talking, explaining what had happened with the details she knew. She told them of coming home after going to the store which, of course, was not close. She told them that she had just spent a little time in town. She then told them about when she had come home finding Michael gone, and then the assailant, his death, Alan, and all the rest. She ended telling them about Alan waiting for the cleanup crew. Melody took notes, Alex just listened, and in the end, they all looked at each other a little perplexed.

"So, do you think they just loaded him in a truck and took him out of there?" Melody asked Abby.

"There were no other ways in," Abby replied to Melody. "I would have seen a helicopter, and they would have still been close if it were a pack out. Alan discovered there was an empty van on a hill from triangulating their coordinates, but I doubt anyone has checked it out, and we eliminated the group of them near the house."

Abby thought for a second and Melody broke in. "So where to go?"

Abby looked at Melody and said, "The thought would be Jackson, or similar, to get a plane."

Melody considered. "Alan is looking into that," she told Abby.

Abby stood. "Then let's get the Scotsman ready, Melody, and we will head east towards Grand Rapids, then change as necessary."

Jay walked up holding his dirty rag, smiling. "Howdy, Alex. Howdy, Melody. Get what you wanted Abby?"

"Yep," Abby said, "but I am going to borrow the Scotsman," she told Jay.

"Umm," Jay said, "I missed where that was part of the plan."

Abby smiled at Jay and made an innocent look as she batted her eyelashes. "Don't trust me?" she asked.

Jay laughed nervously. "Well, it's not that, it's just that, well, you know, she is kinda' the only thing in my life that, well, yeah, I trust you, but hey," he mumbled to Abby.

Abby walked up and hugged Jay. "They will let you fly the

G650 to the Scotsman, right Alex?" she asked.

Jay smiled. "This little thing, why would I want to, hmm, well, that may be fun."

Abby looked impatient, "Mel, when you are ready, let's go. Let's call Alan and see where he is and where we need to be."

Melody stopped. "Before we go, I would like to know what the plan is, as it appears you are ahead here somehow," she told Abby.

Abby looked serious as Alex and Jay looked on. "No, I am not ahead, I am just being driven. I want to get moving. I am not sure where we will end up, but we can't do anything from here. Alan may find something, but he may not. We will be heading to a small town outside of Grand Rapids, Michigan. We're going to look up a gunsmith that may know where the weapon I have in the plane came from, as well as where the darts were made. If we can get that far, we may be able to track down who has Michael."

Melody looked down at the floor. "You know, all of you take things for granted. I can fly, but that thing?" she said hesitantly.

Jay looked at Melody for a moment and said, "She can fly herself if she needs to, it is no issue. Abby has flown her before, and it will be fine." He looked at Abby with a raised eyebrow. "Right Abby?"

Abby looked thoughtful. "I will take care of her. So, Mel, get your gear, let's go, and we will call Alan on the way. This will be like a spa weekend except no massages and a lot more bullets."

Alex laughed. "Funny."

Jay looked at Alex. "She is serious," he said in a funny tone meant to be cute.

Alex laughed again.

Melody went to the 650 and got out her gear, one duffel. She looked at Alex and asked, "I have my service weapons, I know what we walked into in DC. What do I expect here?"

Alex looked back at Melody. "I am not sure, but you are going to a gunsmith, get whatever you need depending on the situation. We will be one day back," he said.

Abby looked at both Alex and Melody. "We have it covered, or at least I do. I have an extra for you Melody if you need It."

Melody and Abby walked to the Scotsman then, with Jay walking beside Abby, letting her know little things that only he knew. "She won't run hot, and remember that when you are coming in, you need a little more flap than those little planes."

Abby stopped, looked at him, and said, "Jay, make sure I don't get blindsided. I will take care of your plane. Take care of my back."

"Got it," Jay said laughing with a belly laugh. "Reminds me of a bar I went to once in Singapore," he said to Abby.

Abby rolled her eyes. "Later," she said as she walked up the ramp. Jay sat at the base of the ramp as Abby lifted the back gate. He looked like someone was stealing his puppy.

As the door closed, Abby opened the trunk of the DB9 and told Melody, "Drop your bag in here." She then closed the truck and they walked to the cockpit.

Melody looked at her as Abby got in the pilot's chair.

"Seems big," she said.

"It is big, but it is like a big puppy. It will be just fine. Strap in and hold on," Abby told Melody.

Melody got strapped in and grabbed a small clipboard to the side of her. "Checklist?" she asked Abby.

Abby replied to Melody, "Yep, let's read it off." The two girls walked through the checklist quickly, and Abby started one engine and began coasting to the end of the hanger area. "This will be fun," Abby said.

Melody looked at her and said, "Your idea and my idea of fun may be a little different."

Abby smiled. "Maybe, and we are about to find out."

Chapter 16

Alan was working diligently, checking on each and every airport within five hundred miles, to determine any plane that may be at least a little nefarious. As he did so, he found that there were a lot of planes in the area that looked quite nefarious. He was pretty sure he had found at least ten drug planes, half a dozen other smuggling operations, and at least four human trafficking planes. He had to look close but did not think they would have dressed Michael up like a girl. He also found a dozen or so planes that were just going up to hang around with someone in the air, and four that made him look twice. Of particular interest was a plane coming out of the Jackson Hole airport with little information, and when he was able to get camera footage in the area, there was a white van that drove up at the last minute before takeoff.

Alan passed some information over to law enforcement as anonymous tips, while he worked his best to trace every plane. He had particular interest in the Lear Jet he now thought Michael was on. He was also a little concerned about the human trafficking planes, wondering how things would turn out.

Alan was quick on his keyboard and finally got access to the flight plans for the Lear Jet. He quickly grabbed his phone and dialed Melody.

"Hello," he heard Melody say with a little static.

"Mel?" Alan asked. "Where are you?"

"Taking off with Abby," Mel told Alan. "Hang on." Alan heard a lot of noise and then a little quiet for a moment and realized they were off the ground. "Alan, yeah, we are in the air, and Abby has this without me. I miss you. Did you find anything?"

Alan said, "Yes, but where are you going?"

"Grand Rapids, Michigan," Melody said, "to follow up on a weapon."

Alan smiled to himself. Abby was driven, and they had determined that was a good place to start. "Okay, that may be good. The plane that I think has Michael on it is headed for Muskegon, Michigan," Alan said.

"I have been to Muskegon," Melody told Alan. "What would be there?"

"Don't count the area out. There are a lot of people around there with money. On the coast are some of the best views in the world. Just because it is not a bad place, doesn't mean there aren't bad people there," Alan told Melody.

Melody scowled and was glad it didn't go over the phone. "I know, Alan. I just was not sure what would be there that would be a good cover."

The line started to have static again. "I will look into things in that area and see what I can find. It may be obvious or well hidden. Muskegon could be a drop point for a dozen other places as well. There are a lot of small cities up there and a lot of countryside to get lost in. There are also many old factories and warehouses that could be used as cover. I will see what I can find." The static was getting heavier. "You know how I feel about you Mel," Alan finished.

"Yeah, me too," Melody said to Alan. The connection dropped. Melody closed the phone and looked over at Abby. "Phone died, but Alan thinks he has the plane, and it's heading for Muskegon, Michigan."

Abby smiled. "Nice place. Michael went there a few years ago to look at some property. There were entire areas having issues and he was able to get a good section of beachfront. I am not sure what he did with it. The property was to the north of Muskegon, but we flew in there. A lot of good people there. Of course, there are some troubled people too, but Michael likes smaller towns, and except for the shopping, I do as well," she told Melody.

Melody looked pensive at Abby. "I am sure it is nice. I did not get anything else from Alan for now. We can check in when we land."

Abby looked at Melody in a matter-of-fact way. "You can use that phone or log on to the hotspot and use the phone through the signal Jay broadcasts. The info is on the clipboard. It won't matter much. We have a destination, and we are on our way. I will land in Grand Rapids. When we can we will head to the west. If we land this in Muskegon it will be a telltale of us being there."

Melody looked at Abby and said, "This is pretty hard to hide."

"It is easier to hide a big plane in the summer. They have some airshows in Muskegon, or they used to have them. Story was someone got political, and it messed things up. It is bad when people get that way and try to make something better that is already good," Abby said to Melody.

Melody looked at Abby and said, "I get you love Michael, but Alex and his team are better equipped to handle this situation. I mean, I'm part of that team. Don't you think it would have been better to involve them?"

Abby banked the plane a little and checked a gauge. "That's a good theory," she told Melody. "Personally, I think the truth is a little different. Alex is used to barging in and solving issues with force. Michael was always patient. Alan is like that too. Anyway, I am not some silly heartsick girl worried about my boyfriend.

Michael and I, well, we share something I like to think is special."

"Special how?" Melody asked Abby.

"Easy," Abby said. "We don't compete with each other. Well, we do, but it is just in fun. You see, we talked about it years ago when we were just friends. Michael was dating my best friend Madison at the time. She was nice but a bit of a flake when it came to love."

"A flake?" Melody asked Abby.

"Yeah, she always wanted to be one step ahead, you know?" Abby asked Melody in a questioning manner.

Melody smiled as Abby banked the plane. "I know the type," she said. "I have met quite a few of them in my life. Always wanting to push themselves up by taking someone else down. It was always worse when they were dating."

Abby was looking forward and checking instruments, but she continued. "Michael and I have never been like that. We started as friends. I never initially saw him in a romantic way, and I don't think he saw me that way either. Instead, we just enjoyed each other's company. When Madison broke his heart, I comforted him, but we stayed as friends for a while. Then one day we just were more, and it was a lot more," Abby shared with Melody.

"What do you mean?" Melody asked Abby.

Abby smiled a distant smile. "It wasn't just a friendship; it was more like a partnership. When we first kissed, it wasn't awkward or strange. It was like an extension of what we were doing. We both were so in tune with each other that we just wanted to give and make the other happy. It became almost like a dance with who would make the other happiest. The first time we had sex, I thought the building was going to explode!" Abby told Melody.

"I know what you mean," Melody said to Abby. "That happens sometimes with me."

Abby turned and looked at Melody. "I am sure, and I am happy you have felt it. The thing that was different and is different with Michael is it doesn't fade. Each day is more than an adventure. There are no doubts, no self-centered introspection, nothing. Instead, we just love each other, wholly and fully. It is not a "when it is convenient" thing. We love each other to the fullest extent of our being each and every day."

Melody smiled just a little. "Not even a fight?" she asked Abby.

Abby laughed. "Oh, Michael and I can fight, but we don't," she told Melody. "I never tire of him, and I trust him with everything I am, and he feels the exact same way about me."

Melody looked out the front of the plane. "Wow. That much trust, no secrets," she said in awe to Abby.

"Didn't say that either," Abby said. "We have our secrets, but if we ask each other, we will tell. There is just nothing that important. We keep finances separate, but if I ask Michael, he will tell me exactly how much money he has at any time. We have a past, but if he asks, I will tell, and if I ask, he will tell. I know it may seem strange, but like I said, every day is an adventure," she told Melody.

Melody smiled again, "I am trying to get used to that concept. Alan is different from anyone I have ever known. Every time I melt away a little more, there seems to be another iceberg underneath."

Abby checked a gauge then said, "There's one that might be a challenge."

Melody laughed and asked Abby, "Why? I know Alan has a past, but he is a good guy."

Abby smiled and replied, "No, Alan is a great guy. I don't think many people will ever get to know him and we barely know him well ourselves. He gave Michael a gift that I don't think anyone could ever give a person without really caring. He was someone that I never expected to do what he did. When we finally met him, we found out that he had been watching over Michael for years."

"Really, how?" Melody asked Abby.

"Michael would always get these weird little messages on his computer," Abby started, as she pulled the yoke back a little to increase the plane's altitude. "He tried for years to track down the person who was sending them, but he never could quite get them. The addresses and IPs seemed to change all the time. Michael is talented on computers, but no expert. In the end, he just stopped worrying about it. The messages always helped or pointed out something Michael should have paid attention to, so it was just not a big deal," she told Melody.

"So, what happened?" Melody asked Abby.

Abby asked Melody, "Do you know how Michael met Alex?"

"Not really," Melody replied to Abby. "Some mission, and Michael was in the middle of it?"

"Yeah, that works," Abby said. "Michael just wanted to be left alone, and we were happy in his house just outside of Ivel, Kentucky. Michael had someone get to our house though, and Alex followed the person thinking Michael was a threat. He was on orders and all, and Michael laughed about and still laughs about it. Michael was reluctant but, in the end, it was a necessity that Michael solve an issue. In the process, he and Alex kind of bonded a little. The entire situation brought up some unresolved issues about his mother and father, Michael's that is. So, Alan revealed himself, and in one quick move took away something Michael had worried about for years. Since then, we see each other from time to time, and the dogs check on us probably daily."

"Probably?" Melody asked Abby.

"Well, sometimes we see them, and sometimes Michael just knows the dogs are there when we don't see them," Abby told Melody.

"Yeah, they are good dogs," Melody said to Abby.

Abby laughed. "The first time I saw them I was with friends in a café in Dubois. This friend said, "Woof," and through a window in a car outside, the dogs both turned and looked at her like they could see inside her soul. It freaked her out, but I laughed about it for a long time. We saw them later the same day and they were a little more forceful."

Melody was still staring out the front window of the giant plane. "He trains the dogs every day. It's not like a real training though. He just works with them, and they work with him. It's almost like they are trying to teach him too," Melody said to Abby about Alan.

Abby looked over at Melody. "Really?" Abby paused for a moment, "Anyway, this conversation has bounced all over."

Melody laughed. "They usually do," she said to Abby. "I like listening, it makes me a good investigator, but I may never understand you and Michael and this whole thing."

Abby smiled as she focused on the gauges in front of her for a moment. "Why not?" she asked Melody.

Melody continued. "In my world, Michael should be in jail. I mean, he has killed people, and the murders were not sanctioned by the government. He may never face justice for it either. At the same time though, you and he get along perfectly, and you seem to have no issue with that."

Abby looked over at Melody with a thoughtful grin. "You forget who my father is, Melody. I have seen death or known about it since I was young, and dear old dad never shielded me from the pain of it all. He thought being honest was best. He was so brutally honest with me, that I was worried if I could have a good relationship with anyone."

Melody looked sad. "I had that too," she told Abby. "My father brought me up hard core Army style. He didn't want me to be a wimp."

Abby laughed. "Well, you know it makes dating hard when your date is worried you might beat them up. Everyone I was growing up with knew who my dad was in the service. The first time a boy tried to hold my hand, I put him in a wrist lock and hurt him. I didn't mean to, but he grabbed me a little quickly, and dad was always saying, "Don't think, do." Well, I did, and the whole school was pissed at me for a month."

"Pissed at you, why?" Melody asked Abby.

"He was Captain of the football team, I was a cheerleader, and I sprained his wrist," Abby said. "He was apologetic, but no boy wanted to talk to me for a long time."

Melody started laughing. "You beat up a football player accidently? When was this?" she asked Abby in a lighthearted tone.

"Ninth grade," Abby smiled.

"Wow! The start of high school. That had to be rough," Melody said to Abby.

"A little," Abby replied, "but it also got me a lot of respect, so I never had to worry about people treating me badly. In the end, it was tolerable," Abby told Melody.

Melody as once again thoughtful with a sly knowing grin on her face. "I had a similar experience, but I was taller and bigger than most of my classmates," she told Abby. "I was a real tomboy, thanks to my family. When we were in the middle of the school year one year, I decided to be a tough girl and try to wrestle. Girls were allowed, but none ever applied because the coach always paired them with someone bigger who could beat them. Well, I got on the team, and he paired me with Jimmy Sagemiller. Jimmy was a really big guy, but he was nice to me, and the coach was pushing him for a submission. Jimmy tried to do what the coach wanted, saying he was sorry every time, but he also realized it was not as easy as he thought. I ended up putting him in a submission hold and he tapped out."

Abby laughed and asked Melody, "What happened?"

Melody smiled. "We dated through high school, of course. He was always trying to protect me, but never needed to do so," she told Abby.

Abby hit a few switches and leaned back as the autopilot took over. "So, what about wrestling?" she asked Melody.

"Won the division my Senior year, and eventually the coach was on my side," Melody answered.

"I bet," Abby said, and looked at a small screen to her side.

"We have about two and a half hours to Grand Rapids. If you want to stretch or change, you can. Looks like it is warm, but I know the weather can change quickly there. Not bad, but the nights can be cool. If you haven't eaten, Jay keeps a stocked fridge in the main hold. He used to pretty much live on this thing. If you are okay, I want to talk, but I need to take at least a 30-minute nap. Too much stuff happening, and I talked the whole way with Jay so I need it," she told Melody.

"Boring you?" Melody asked.

"No, just being honest," Abby said. "Getting some rest is something Michael and I believe in fully."

"Thanks," Melody said. "I was just kidding. I am good for now though. Why don't you take your nap, and I will keep an eye on things?" she said.

"Thanks," Abby laughed. "I shouldn't be long, but the beds on this thing are nice and you know how that goes."

Melody laughed. "I have been on one, they suck," she replied to Abby.

Abby smirked. "Not this one." She went behind the cockpit only a few feet and folded out the bed. The standard beds on the plane seemed quite normal, but as she folded this one out, the memory foam mattress could be seen. She pulled a pillow and a quilt out of a cupboard and got on the floating cot."

Melody looked back and said, "Damn, Abby, that's nicer than what I have been on in these monsters."

Abby laughed. "Like I said, Jay pretty much lived on this thing."

Melody looked at Abby with a twinkle in her eye, "Sleep fast." She then checked the controls and left the autopilot on and simply scanned the horizon. To the north, she saw a storm and knew Abby had come through it. She thought about asking about the storm but decided to leave it for later. Through the left window, she watched the lightning bounce on the horizon and wondered how Alan was, if he was okay. She shook the thought out of her head and looked to the east. "Always look forward and find your way every day," she thought as she watched.

Chapter 17

Jim was focused. His brow was furled in utter concentration. Rachel stood next to him, supportively. He was ready. He lined up, pulled back his arm, and the dice rolled from his fingers, bouncing along the green velvet surface of the table.

"Seven!" the stickman announced. "Another winner, another chicken dinner!" Jim jumped up laughing and Rachel hugged him. The stack of chips was impressive.

Ronnie came up to him, with Barbara locked on his arm with Terry following slightly behind. "Jim, that's a big stack," he stated. "Should you like take some back or something?"

The stickman pushed the dice back to Jim and said, "Place your bets."

A large crowd of people were around Jim and the group as he played craps. Jim looked at Ronnie, thought for a second, and reached down and took half the chips and put them in front of him. "Good idea," he said. He then picked up the dice and had Rachel blow on them. There was still no point for Jim was up. He was actually way up. The bets were locked, and he rolled the dice again.

The red cubes bounced along the table and seemed alive, as they randomly popped from side to side then rolled and slowed. "Seven!" the stickman said again. "The winner's a winner, the losers are losers. The table is hot if you back the winner."

Jim smiled, looked at Ronnie, and took half of the chips off the table again. Barbara kissed Ronnie on the ear, and he jumped as he looked excitedly at the table. "Happy?" Jim said, looking at Ronnie.

"Yes, sir," Ronnie said. "My dad always told me that if you

are winning, improve your luck by holding something back."

Jim smiled. "Ronnie, you are a gem," he said wryly.

Rachel nudged Jim. The dice had come back, and he sat with money on the table. He did not count the money when he was playing because he was fond of not knowing. That, and it always made him miss a little.

The stickman was repeating, "Place your bets!"

Jim said, "We are good," and then he let Rachel blow on the dice and threw them another time. This time two fours came up on the dice.

"A square pair!" came the yell from the stickman as he pushed the dice back.

Jim looked down, saw the two stacks of chips in front of him and the stack on the table. He smiled and picked up the dice, let Rachel blow on them again, and rolled them in his hand. He looked up and threw the dice on the table. They bounced wildly for a moment, slowed, rolled once then twice, then stopped again on two fours.

"Eight the hard way, winner!" the stickman barked.

The Boxman looked at Jim dryly while the dealer paid out his bet. Jim reached down and picked up all the chips and waved his hands. The stickman barked, "The shooter's done, he takes his luck, the shooters done he got a buck."

Jim laughed and looked at Ronnie and told him, "I always play just to hear the stickmen. They are always so colorful."

"Yeah, he's a funny guy," Ronnie said.

Jim held a tray of chips and said, "What now?"

Rachel was looking at her phone and said simply, "I guess we are heading back to the hanger, Jim."

"We just got here," Jim replied a little sadly to Rachel.

"Alex says to meet at the hanger, as soon as possible," Rachel told Jim.

"I guess that puts this party down," Jim shrugged. "Let me cash in, Rachel."

As Jim and the group walked to the cashier, three men walked up next to Jim and one of them said, "Sir, my name is Arthur. We work for the Casino. We would enjoy it if we could comp your stay here and upgrade you to a suite of your liking."

Jim smiled. He had no idea how much he had won, but it appears he had won more than a little. "Thanks, we have to leave for a while, but we will be back. Can I take a rain-check on that?" he asked Arthur.

"Certainly," Arthur said quietly. "I will give you my card. When you come back, ask for me and I will ensure you and your group are well taken care of."

Jim glanced at the card that Arthur handed him and said, "Thank you."

"No problem, sir," Arthur responded to Jim. Arthur then walked around the cashier stands and through a set of doors to the cashier area. He walked up to where Jim was at and waited. Jim handed over the chips and the woman counted through them and handed him a sheet.

"What's this?" Jim asked.

"It is for your player's card," Arthur answered Jim. "You don't need to fill everything out. Just write down your name, phone number and email address, for a start."

Jim smiled. "I have one on file. Not necessary," he told Arthur.

The woman who had counted Jim's chips asked, "Cash or certified check?"

"Cash is fine," Jim told the woman.

The woman started pulling out stacks of money and then began counting to Jim. "20, 40, 60, 80, 100 thousand dollars," the woman said. She then broke open every stack and checked the amount of each 10-thousand-dollar pack as Jim smiled. It took several minutes but she finished, then brought out a small leather bag which she put the bills in. She tied the top of the bag and handed it to Jim. "Congratulations, sir," the woman said to Jim as Ronnie looked on in awe.

"Boss is getting antsy," Terry said to the group. "We should go."

Jim spun around and walked towards the door with the other four in tow. The two men in suits walked them out and asked for a limo to be brought up. Jim looked at them. "Compliments of the house," they told him.

"Thanks," Jim said to the men.

"Where to?" the limo driver asked as Jim and the others got in the big vehicle.

"Airport," Jim replied to the driver." "The private hanger area."

The man smiled. "Yes, sir," he said to Jim.

"Oh my god!" Rachel screamed. "You just won a hundred thousand dollars! How much did you start with?" she asked Jim.

Jim smiled and told Rachel, "I put down a thousand on the first roll."

"That was quite a run, Jim," Terry said. "You don't see that every day."

"No, I have missed out on it," Jim told Terry. "Must have been Rachel."

"Jim," Ronnie said, "you sure are lucky."

Jim looked out the window and his demeanor changed. "Guys, not the way to the airport." "Where we going?" Jim asked the driver.

"Airport," the driver responded, making a sharp turn into an alleyway. "The long way."

The limo driver pulled the car over and four guys came to the doors and opened them. "Out!" they yelled.

Jim and the group got out quickly and pushed back the man holding the door. The biggest man Jim recognized. "You work at the casino," he stated.

"No duh, asshole," the man said to Jim. "Now hand over the cash and you can get on your way."

One man held a baseball bat, three had knives and one was

unarmed. Jim looked at the big man from the casino and the driver who was now next to him. "You sure you wanna' do this?" he asked the men.

"Give us the money then you can go. No one will believe you about anything you say since you are out of towners being stupid," the driver told Jim.

Rachel started laughing at the driver. Terry stepped to the side and Barbara grabbed Ronnie's arm, but Ronnie stepped forward. Jim laughed and handed the bag to Barbara. He winked at her. The driver stepped forward and Jim did as well, but as he stepped forward, he spun and swept his leg under the driver. The driver fell with a loud "thunk."

Rachel was moving right away. At 6'3 she was a formidable woman, but it was not her height that made her that way. She took the man closest to her and hit him once in the throat while she kicked forward at the second man. They both fell to the ground. Three men down in the first few seconds.

Jim stopped, ran his hand through his hair and looked at the last two men standing. The man from the casino looked at his friends on the ground and anger flared. He reached behind his back and pulled out a pistol. However, as he did, there was a pop in the air and it flew from his hand. Terry stood to the back holding a Glock 19 with an AAC silencer. The man grasped his now bleeding hand.

Barbara spoke up. "I know you guys are having fun, but we really need to get back to the plane. Alex has texted 8 times."

Jim walked up to the man who just tried to rob him. "Sorry, I wanted to play, and so did she," as he looked over at Rachel, "but we have to work," he said. Then he told Barbara to take a picture and told her, "We will let the fine men of the LVPD have this young man, as he really wants to turn himself in."

Barbara snapped a picture, and Rachel walked up to the man sitting there holding his hand. He was defiant, but she looked right into his eyes and told him, "You are a lucky bastard. You may never know who you just tried to fuck with." The man's demeanor changed. He looked stunned.

Terry got in behind the steering wheel of the limo and told the driver, "By the way, we are taking your car. It will be at the airport." The five got in the car and were soon out of the alley and on their way to the hanger.

Chapter 18

Michael laughed on the inside. Most people have never thought about acting as if they are unconscious. There is a trick to it that only few ever master. Skiers are told to go limp in a tumble as it will allow them to survive more easily. Yogis can put themselves in a trance that allow them to act paralyzed. It is daunting how the subtlest moves can be perceived, so Michael worked hard to perfect looking as if he's in an unconscious state.

The hardest thing for Michael, while faking being unconscious, turned out to be when the guards went to put shorts on him. People just don't realize how you try to help when others are putting clothes on you. It was made extremely difficult as neither of the men were very articulate. They continued to miss the leg hole of the shorts and put two feet in one. In the end, the guards finally managed to get the shorts on Michael, but they were on backwards.

Michael was put on the floor in the back of a plane with a blanket thrown over him. Once he was covered, he opened his eyes. The material was not super thin, but he could easily make out the two men guarding him and the one man who went to the cockpit. Michael waited.

While the plane was taxiing, Michael had managed to work free of his bindings and released his hands. It cost him a few layers of skin, but he was good. He stayed still but noticed the blood on the blanket and hoped it would not seep through.

Michael heard the tower clear them for take-off and felt the brakes on the plane hold the thrust in place. He continued to wait. The brakes were released, and the plane rocketed forward. Michael's timing would need to be perfect.

The plane was going down the runway faster and faster. Michael heard the wheels on the pavement, the blocks clicking from one to the next. He guessed they were going 80 then 90 miles per hour. As they reached a little over 130 mph, Michael felt the wheels lighten. This is when people on planes hold on and are at their most vulnerable. Michael's legs were still bound, but as the front of the plane lifted from the ground, he slowly worked the covers back and saw the two men.

The first man Michael saw was a black man, probably thirty-five years old. He was a big guy wearing all black tac gear. Michael saw the special forces knife on his side. He also saw weapons, but none were drawn. The second man was about 35, light skinned and red haired. He wore digital camo and had tac gloves of the same design. The lighter skinned man's gear looked brand new. Michael smiled.

As the plane nosed up, the group weighed a little more from the G-force. Michael moved forward. He grabbed the black man and forced his head into the wall, which put him out cold immediately. The redhead looked over and gasped then reached for his weapon. As he drew it, Michael had already pulled the knife from the black man and put it directly through the redhead's knee, effectively pinning him to the chair. The man dropped the gun weakly.

Michael reached to his vest and pulled the reverse hanging knife down. Without removing his eyes from the man, he sliced the zip ties from his feet. Michael was now free.

"Don't kill me," the man said as he cradled his leg.

"Oh, sorry, I left you hanging," Michael said, as he pulled the knife out of the man's femur. Michael no sooner had taken the knife out of the man when he had the blade on his neck. He surveyed the area. No cameras, cockpit door closed. No issues for the moment. "Weapons, please," Michael said to the man.

The man reached with shaky hands and began dropping his weapons. There were not many. A small Berretta Nano fell to the floor first. Michael picked it up. "Nano, huh?" he said to the man. "They should call these "Nono's." I mean, they shoot good, but you should not have one. You should carry something more suitable. I guess this is your backup, but it would be better if you used the PX4 and the associated rifle. Same ammo, easier to deal with, and a good weapon in a pinch." A Glock 19 fell to the floor as well, as Michael kept talking, along with a small butterfly knife.

Michael put the Nano on the floor, checked the black man again, and picked up the Glock and the knife. "Also, nice weapons," he said. "The 19 is great, but man, make up your mind. Who is it you like? Work the mags, boy. You need to be as lightweight and interchangeable as you can." Michael pulled the magazine out of the weapon and started laughing. "These are range rounds. You are a newbie, aren't you? What's your name, red?"

"Ziggs," the man said weakly to Michael. "Tom Ziggs."

"Okay, Ziggs," Michael said. "So, why are you with this group?" he asked.

"Money, sir," Ziggs replied. "I am not good at anything, and this guy was paying 50k a head to guard an unconscious man. I needed the money, bad."

"Why, Ziggs, you a coker, a druggie, some type of player?" Michael asked.

"No, sir," Ziggs said. "My daughter is dying, cancer, but I don't expect you to understand," he told Michael.

Michael laughed. "You don't even know who I am, do you?"

"I was told you're some type of criminal," Ziggs answered.

"Maybe so, but this isn't about the law." Michael looked at the man's pack. "Zip ties?" Michael asked.

"Front pack," Ziggs told Michael.

Michael took several long zip ties from the man's pack and smiled. "I know some tricks with these," he told the man, then went on to say, "Maybe I'll show you another time. Arms on the armrests. Oh, and no yelling, warning or anything else. I know, I know, you didn't think of that, but I did," he said. Michael went on to tie the man's hands down firmly to the armrests, then his legs behind the armrests. It was tight, but it would work for what was necessary.

"Feel okay, Ziggs?" Michael asked.

"Yeah, for being tied up, that is," Ziggs responded to Michael.

Michael went through the rest of Ziggs' packs on his tac vest. He put all the magazines and secondary items on the blanket he had been covered with, then he went to the black man. Working quickly, Michael pulled all the weapons out of the man's vest and disarmed him completely. As he had guessed, this man was much better prepared and would have been the bigger threat. Michael zip tied him to the chair and put a pillow behind his back. As Michael went through the weapons, he found one he was not familiar with. "What's this?" Michael asked about the strange pistol.

"Dart gun," Ziggs said. "We were told it would put people out for hours. They said something about histamines, but I don't know anything about it. They said you should have been out all the way to Michigan."

Michael smiled and asked Ziggs, "How's it work?"

Ziggs told Michael, "You just pull the trigger."

The plane was leveling off now. Michael guessed he only had a few minutes left. He stood up in the cabin and looked down. He was wearing gym shorts, but they were inside out and backwards. "God, don't you boys ever get dressed?" he asked Ziggs.

Ziggs smiled and asked Michael, "Ever try to dress another man while he was naked and you couldn't hold him up?"

"Yeah, staged a scene like that once," Michael replied. "I guess you have to get used to it," he smiled as he stretched.

Ziggs gulped. "What are you going to do?" he asked Michael.

Michael hefted the light dart gun. "I guess I am going to put the pilot out, or at least give him a choice," he answered Ziggs.

Ziggs said fearfully to Michael, "We will crash."

"Well, you can fly, can't you?" Michael asked Ziggs and laughed. "I mean, you can soldier, and guard, so I thought you could fly." Ziggs started crying and Michael grinned. "God, you picked the wrong job," he stated.

Ziggs lowered his head and said to Michael, "I know."

Michael went to the back, found the bags but then heard the cockpit door. He got behind the chair and waited as the pilot walked into the cabin and stopped. Michael stood and pointed the weapon at him. "On the ground!" he barked quickly.

"What?" the man said to Michael.

"Floor, now!" Michael demanded.

The pilot started to back up toward the cockpit. "Damnit, why are you all such idiots?" Michael said as he shot him in the chest. The man fell right away. He went to him then and zip hogtied him. "Is this guy your brother or something?" he asked Ziggs.

"Cousin," Ziggs told Michael.

"Really?" Michael asked Ziggs and smiled. "Where you from?"

"West Virginia," Ziggs said to Michael.

"Damn," Michael said, "Kentucky. Was living around Ivel for a while," he told Ziggs.

"We went hunting there all the time," Ziggs said to Michael.

"Really, where?" Michael asked Ziggs as he went through the pilot's pockets.

Ziggs told Michael, "Up in the hills. There's a lot of boys out there that hunt."

Michael looked at Ziggs, checked the other man, then slapped Ziggs on the cheek playfully. "Gotta check the plane. Be right back." He went to the front and checked the controls. They were at 20,000 feet, cruising on autopilot, with a heading of almost an even 90, due east. He checked the fuel and engines, then went back towards the back.

"You okay, Ziggs?" Michael asked.

"Yeah," Ziggs said. "I am okay."

Michael went to the back of the plane and looked through

bags. He pulled out clothes from two of them, checked sizes, sorted, and grabbed a black t-shirt and put it on. Digging deeper, he found underwear and put those on as well. He then pulled on pants and black socks, and the belt he found he cinched hard, for the pants were a little loose. Michael looked for shoes but there were no extra. He went to the pilot then and checked his shoe size. "God, kid's foot," Michael said and laughed. "What size you wear, Ziggs?"

"10," Ziggs told Michael.

"I need an 11, Michael said to Ziggs. Why does everyone have such small feet?" He laughed.

"Maybe you just have bigger feet," Ziggs said to Michael, laughing but looking white-faced.

"Huh," Michael said to Ziggs, "better check you. I forgot I put a knife in your femur. Well, really I didn't forget, but I have been busy." Ziggs smiled as he looked up at Michael, resembling a pale red-haired ghost. Michael checked Ziggs' leg and took out the knife, ripped his pants up the side, and tied a bandage over the wound. "You will live. Just be cool," Michael said. He then turned and observed the unconscious black man. "He is still out. No conversation there." He checked the man's shoes, size 12. Michael took off the government issue combat boots and put them on his feet. They were a little loose but not bad.

Michael then went back to the luggage and began going through every piece he could find. He finally found a bigger suitcase, and inside was a pair of size 12 tennis shoes. Michael thought his unconscious friend was up for jogging later so he took the shoes back and left them at his feet. "Ziggs," Michael said, "Gotta' fly the plane for a second. Yell if you need me."

Ziggs smiled with a very weak smile and nodded softly.

Michael wondered if he had waited too long to wrap Ziggs' wound, but he didn't really worry about it much. In his mind, he simply thought the man chose the wrong team. As quickly as the thought entered his mind it was gone. He did not have the time or effort to worry about what was going on in someone else's life right now.

Michael sat down in the pilot's chair and started tuning the radio. He listened in for a moment, nothing. He turned on the tower and was about to speak when he heard noises in the cabin. Michael got up in time to see the black man angrily rip off the second zip tie and stand up. The man then slipped in his stocking feet which made him even angrier. Michael laughed and the man rushed him. As the black man reached the cockpit door, Michael let him pass through and he bashed headfirst into the console. This time the man was dazed but not out and struggled to get to Michael. Michael put the man in a wristlock though, and he pushed him to the ground. He then took out the dart gun and said to the man, "Night-night, sweet prince."

As Michael pulled the trigger he heard the man say, "No!" and saw him go limp.

Michael flung the man back into the cabin where he found Ziggs unconscious. He was about to zip tie the black man when he heard the engine sputter so he ran to the front and sat down. He checked the gauges and everything was correct. Then he saw the fuel. He looked to the side and saw the man's impact with the console had hit the fuel dump. There was simply no gas. "Shit," Michael said. He looked at the gauges and the GPS, trying to find his position. He was somewhere over the Shoshone National Forest, and that is where he would be landing, crashing, or otherwise finding himself, in a moment.

Michael looked at the back and saw all three men out cold.

There was no time to do anything, so he left them to whatever happened. Michael extended the flaps and hoped he could float until he could see a road or something. He looked over the horizon, trying to keep his cool, and could not see anything.

The engines went dead. Michael tried to keep the nose up and drift on the wind, but the aircraft was too heavy to drift well without power. Gliders use their huge wings to glide on the wind but also have strict weight limits. This was definitely not a glider.

Michael saw a large field to his north and steered slowly towards it. He tried to slow the plane by diving a little then nosing up. He lost altitude and speed each time he did so. The field was a mile away and he was still going too fast. He needed to slow the plane down so he nosed up hard, pushing the plane forcefully in to the air, and then he eased forward. The wings strained, and the plane strained under the weight, but he got the speed down to under 80 miles per hour. He laughed as he didn't even know what kind of plane he was on and he was trying to fly it.

Easing forward, Michael dropped the plane's gear. They seemed to lock in place but there was an error light on. He thought he should have just shot all three men, no problems then, and this would have been easy. He noted to himself, stop leaving people alive and then he laughed out loud.

When Michael was fifty feet off the ground, he nosed up the plane again and tried to slow down one last time. The wind was kicking up and pushing him to the side and the controls with no engine were sluggish to say the least. He pulled hard, and the plane lurched, stalled slightly, and hit the ground. It rolled for a moment, and then Michael felt the front gear give way. He thought they must have hit a tree or something similar. The plane fell forward and came to an immediate stop, as he heard glass break and objects in the back fall everywhere. Michael hit his head on the yoke, and then everything went black.

Chapter 19

Melody looked out over the horizon as the land below appeared in massive patterns then disappeared. She had always been fascinated by how the land had been worked by farmers and cities alike to be geometric in design when you looked at it from above. It was the farms though that interested her most. In some areas they were near perfect squares from the side. Massive areas that were plowed and turned and planted year after year. In other areas though, the land was tilled in giant circles, most likely so huge sprinkler systems could rotate in their never-ending quest to keep the soil moist and ready for plant growth.

Melody was not an expert pilot like everyone else seemed to be. She actually felt a little out of place in the group with her flying skill. Jim and Alex were both expert pilots. Jim loved to fly and had flown many different types of jets. Alex flew but to him it was purely work. He did not enjoy it, but he knew how and did it very well. Terry and Barbara had both flown jets in the Navy. Though Rachel did not fly, she was intimidating in her own right. She once said, "You guys fly. Just drop me where you want ass kicked."

Ronnie was a mystery to Melody. He was by far the most honest of the group, like only a rural soldier can be. She had tried to talk to him once about flying when they were on a plane to California. He had simply said to her, "If they want me to fly, I will do it. I will do whatever Alex says, for he is my commanding officer, and the General is his. I will make sure I do what I need to do." Melody had smiled at the answer, and when she pressed him, she got a similar one, which made her think that Ronnie was a lot smarter than he let on. She believed that he was more worldly than the group usually gave him credit for.

Of course, in action, Ronnie had never let anyone down. He was clearly always the patience and the conscience of the group, maybe even more so than Alex.

Melody, with her less than perfect flying skills, checked the plane's instrument gauges again. As she went through the dozens of them, she was reminded of a scene in the movie, "Airplane." She snickered expecting to see, "Wash," "Spin," "Rinse," and "A Little Hot" on the board as she checked it. Of course, it was not there, but it was a funny moment for her.

It had been almost an hour since Abby started resting and she looked very peaceful, even with the loud drone of the engines. She was wearing the headset on the bed directly behind the flight cabin. Melody considered this young lady who was dating, living with, and very dedicated to a very proficient assassin. She looked at Abby, sleeping like an innocent. Her small frame seemed so helpless, and her curled blond hair so perfect. If it was not for the fact that she too was a very proficient fighter in her own right, Melody would have thought her a Barbie doll. Melody amused herself again as she thought about a Barbie with accessories like a P90 fully automatic rifle and an FN5.7 handgun. She wondered if they could get the hand grenade or the missile launcher additions to the set and she laughed out loud.

Abby's eyes opened and focused on Melody. "What's so funny?" Abby asked.

"Nothing," Melody said to Abby with a smile, looking out at the horizon again.

"Well c'mon, spill," Abby told Melody with a yawn.

"No, really," Melody said to Abby. "It's nothing."

Abby pressed Melody. "Okay, I need to wake up anyway. Tell me what's so funny," she said while she got out of the bed, folding it easily into the side of the frame of the cockpit. Abby then worked her way to the pilot's chair.

Melody looked over at Abby and said to her, "I was just thinking. You are so perfect, like a Barbie, and I was wondering if there was a Commando Barbie?"

Abby started laughing and said to Melody, "Well, officially there isn't one, but there is one made by Michael for me. It is at the house. You will have to ask me about it sometime and I will show you. He had the weapons and the outfits made for a Barbie and had it made up just like me. I laughed so hard I cried when he gave it to me. It was one of the best presents ever."

"Really?" Melody asked Abby. "I have gotten a lot of good gifts but never something with that much thought in it."

"He made it worse," Abby said. "It came with a daddy figure, my dad, all done up with his dress uniform on. It was a funny combination," she told Melody.

Melody laughed and said "Okay, so my imagination was outdone. I will admit it," she said to Abby.

Abby smiled. "Michael pays a lot of attention and tries to give me something that will melt my heart," she said to Melody. "I can have anything I want, money wise, and really don't want or need anything. So, he thinks of fun things to do."

Melody laughed again. "Wow, lucky girl! I had someone give me a vacuum cleaner for Christmas once. I was like, "Trying to sweep me off my feet?" she told Abby.

Abby laughed at what Melody said and responded, "Yeah, lots of people go through life thinking that stuff makes a relationship work. That is so goofy. Lots of people don't pay attention to their partner. If they only took a moment and did so, both lives would be complete. I mean, the biggest reasons most people have problems are due to money and sex. I don't think we will ever want for money, and well, if either of us asked, the other would always be ready for sex. As it is, I think we are still 18 years old sometimes. When that becomes unimportant, most relationships just fizzle."

Melody looked at Abby a little differently for a moment. What she had seen was a young girl who was in a grown-up world but had unique skills. Now she saw that Abby is actually very mature for her age, the blue eyes showing a lifetime of experience and thought. "Abby, you are an old soul," Melody said.

Abby laughed. "An old almost thirty, huh?" she said to Melody.

"You know what I mean," Melody told Abby.

"Yeah, thanks," Abby said. "We need to start our decent soon. Do you want to change before we land?" she asked Melody.

Melody got up from the tight cockpit and stretched, answering Abby, "Yeah, I think I will. It has been a long day."

Abby checked gauges and looked at Melody and told her, "Yeah, and it may be a long night."

Melody worked her way to the back of the plane and got in the trunk of the DB9. Her bag was well organized. She pulled out a new tank top, a new blue button-down shirt and a pair of jeans. She undressed in the large area in front of the car and marveled at the size of the plane. The specs for the plane had it as easily carrying three vehicles. The relatively small DB9 looked very little in this large area. As Melody put the shirt on, she felt refreshed and alive. She wondered how the day would go. She looked at her boots as she put them back on, stopped, went back to the trunk, and she got out a pair of Sketcher tennis shoes. She felt that they might fit a little better than army issue combat boots.

Once dressed, Melody walked back up to the cabin and sat back in the copilot chair. She put on the headset and looked over at Abby, who was now talking to the Grand Rapids tower. As she listened, she learned that Alex had apparently made arrangements for a hanger for them once she landed, and Abby was getting ground instructions. She then lined up for her turn to land.

"Well, that was quick," Abby said. "Let's see if we can land this monster."

"What?" Melody asked with a little terror in her voice. "You have landed this before, right, Abby?"

Abby smiled. "Not this plane, but a few bigger. It will be just fine," she told Melody.

Melody tightened her seatbelt in the copilot's chair. "Checklist?" she asked Abby.

Abby nodded and Melody pulled out a small clipboard and started going down a list of items. They adjusted flaps and speed and were lining up perfectly. Abby smiled again. "No pressure, huh?"

"No," Melody said. "What's the worst that could happen?" she said jokingly to Abby.

"Nothing big," Abby responded to Melody. "We could just smear our lipstick down the runway and ruin Jay's paint job or explode in a fiery ball of flame."

"Nice thought." Melody laughed. "You are kidding, right?" she asked Abby.

Abby giggled and said to Melody, "Flaps," and she gave them two notches on the flaps.

The sun was behind the plane as it descended into the airport. Abby and Melody could see the incredible blue of lake Michigan some 45 miles behind them. Then they could no longer see it as they went lower and lower. The ground came up and the plane touched down effortlessly. As the plane slowed, Melody smiled.

"I have landed this plane a dozen times," Abby grinned. "It was fun seeing you sweat though!" she told Melody.

Melody looked at Abby, paused, looked forward, looked at her again and said, "Bitch!" in a terse tone.

Abby looked over at Melody and said with a smile, "You say that like it's a bad thing."

Melody looked at Abby again and they both started laughing as the plane slowed and Abby made the turn towards the hangers. The ground traffic was light. She did not have to stop, and as she pulled to the waiting hanger a fuel truck met her there. "Ready for this?" Abby asked Melody.

Abby and Melody unbuckled and got out of the cockpit and Abby walked to the back and lowered the ramp. As she walked down it, she was met by two men looking at the plane and they said, "Nice picture!"

Abby laughed. "The Happy Scotsman appreciates that. Go ahead and fill the tanks. I will cover it," she told the men.

"It's paid for," one of the men told Abby. "We got the call to fill it up about an hour ago, and we are supposed to check fluids and advise a guy named Jay at a number we were given."

Abby smiled and looked at Melody. "Alex thinks of everything."

"Did you need any help, ma'am?" one of the men asked Abby.

"Nope, just close her up when you are done," Abby told the man, then pointed down to Melody. She went back up to the plane and the men heard the throaty roar of the DB9. Abby backed it down the ramp and then pulled to a stop. "Thanks, guys," she said as Melody got in, then asked, "and where is the exit?" One of the men pointed to a gate a few hundred yards away. She saw the sign that said exit. "Duh," she said. "Thanks again." Abby pressed the gas and the car leapt forward like a ready predator. It was time to get busy and find Michael.

Chapter 20

Jay was pacing. It had been nearly three hours since they had arrived and the team was not back at the plane. He knew why Alex waited. He did not want people of action sitting at a plane waiting to leave, but he now questioned the decision since it had taken so long for a short drive. The team was supposedly at Caesars, but it was over 90 minutes since Alex called for them to return. They had plenty of time to get there.

The limo drove up at that very moment and Jay looked actually relieved. As the 5 piled out of the limo with Jim driving, Alex looked at him and said, "Nice of you to get here."

Jim laughed. "Probably my fault," he told Alex.

Rachel quickly cut him off and said, "Fuck that, it was not your fault, Jim. Alex, we just got jumped by some wannabe fruitcakes that wanted to rob us."

Ronnie smiled. "Yes, sir, they were not very nice men," he told Alex.

Barbara hugged Ronnie and he blushed as usual.

Alex looked perplexed. "We need to be in the air, like now."

Jay scurried up the steps, which looked strange because of his size. He quickly and efficiently got into the pilot's chair.

As Terry Drake, the normal pilot, got on the plane, he looked at the cockpit and asked, "What is this?"

Alex frowned. "I made a deal, and he gets to fly," he told Terry.

Terry looked at Alex then and said, "I am responsible for this plane, and it is not some piece of junk anyone can fly."

Jay turned around and asked Terry, "You calling my plane a piece of junk?"

Terry turned red. "Well, no, I have flown the Hercules, but it is not the same type of plane," he said to Jay.

Jay turned around again as he went through preflight. "I am qualified on the Raptor and the Falcon, and I got to fly the Blackbird for 20 minutes once. This is not quite of that caliber, but it will be fun."

Terry looked at Alex with unsure eyes. It was the first time Alex had ever seen Terry show much emotion about the plane. "Can I copilot, at least," he asked almost timidly.

Jay looked back. "Absolutely! Get up here Terry. Let's do some flying, Scotsman style!"

Terry sat down next to Jay in the copilot's seat and began checking the instruments. The two worked through the checklist quickly while Alex talked to Jim. "What happened?" he asked.

"I had a run of luck at the casino," Jim answered Alex. "I won a hundred thousand dollars. Well, a few guys took us down a dark alley and wanted to take it from us. Rachel and I took care of them. I don't think anyone is dead, but we called the police, and they are on their way. We also called the casino and told them that their employee was targeting winners. I am sure he may die, but it won't be on us," Jim rambled off.

"God, I can't let you guys go anywhere. I mean, does trouble just naturally follow you?" Alex asked Jim.

"I think it just likes us, and that includes you too. It may be a little like a boyfriend girlfriend thing, maybe a 'friends with benefits' affair," Jim said, smiling at Alex.

"Yeah, I am worried we are about to be up to our neck in bullshit again," Alex told Jim quietly.

"Me too," Jim said. "Did anyone track down the plane Michael was supposed to be on?" he asked Alex.

"I have not heard yet," Alex told Jim, one engine began to whine and Alex heard his phone ring. Alex picked it up quickly, "Hello?"

"Alex, this is Alan," came a voice. "I am pretty sure I traced the plane that Michael was on, but it has gone off the radar."

"What does that mean?" Alex asked Alan.

"It means that the plane disappeared somewhere around Yellowstone," Alan told Alex.

"This just keeps getting better," Alex said to Alan.

"Ideas?" Alan asked Alex.

Alex thought for a moment. Jim was next to him, and he asked, "What's up, boss?"

"The plane Alan thought Michael was on has dropped off the grid," Alex informed Jim.

"That ain't good," Jim said. "If we book, we can be there in under 2 hours," he told Alex.

Alex thought and said to Jim, "We have too many wheels turning here and we keep splitting things up."

Alan, still on the phone, broke in. "It is somewhere in the Mink Creek area. It is only about 150 miles, but it will not be an easy trek. It is in the middle of nowhere and they could have just gone low to avoid radar. I have seen weirder."

Alex thought for a second. "Helicopter?" he asked Alan.

"I can use a plane and fly over," Alan said after thinking about it. "If I see something, I can get help. I am not sure what else we can do. You deal with finding who started this, I will try to track the plane," he told Alex.

Jim was trying to listen in. "I can head that way," he told Alex.

Alex looked at Jim. "It is an eight-hour drive or a lot of that to charter a plane and do the necessary work. Not a good use of our time. Let's let Alan look at it, we have nothing to lose. We know where Abby is going, but we don't have a good idea of what she is walking into though."

Jim sat down in the front seat. Barbara moved to the back and sat near Ronnie, while Rachel spread herself out on a few chairs.

Alex closed the door and told Alan, "Do what you can and advise when possible."

Alan said, "Will do, and the line went dead."

Alex sat down and said to Jim, "Maybe we are getting too old to deal with Masterson stuff."

Jim laughed. "I tried to get out at the start of all this crap, but you and that General guy made me come back," he told Alex.

Alex laughed. "Speaking of which, I should call the General and let him know what is going on," he said to Jim.

Jim laughed harder. "I do not want to hear that phone call." He made his voice sound higher and said, "and then I let your daughter go alone with another girl in the middle of a kidnapping with more than 8 people dead already." He laughed again and spoke normally. "How's that going to go for you?" he asked Alex.

The second engine began whining and the two now created a chorus of their own special whine and Jay yelled back, "Y'all ready for this?"

Terry yelled, "Say no!"

Jay closed the door to the cockpit, and they felt the plane taxi out to the runway. They stopped, and Alex and Jim heard Terry say "no" even through the door. The engines whined hard, and the plane seemed to be stuck in place while they got louder and louder. Suddenly everyone was thrown against the back of their chairs as the plane rocketed down the runway. After a very short time, the plane then shot almost straight up. As it went up, propelled by what had to be full thrust, it spun at least twice before leveling out well above the air traffic.

The intercom came on. "Alex, he's nuts," Terry said.

Then the intercom came on again. "The previous statement was brought to you by Captain Chicken Little. Welcome to 25,000 feet. We will be cruising here for a little while, while Captain Little cools his jets." Alex, Jim and Rachel heard the voice in the background saying, "You are an asshole," and then the intercom went off.

Alex laughed, Jim laughed harder, and Rachel asked if they could do it again. This was going to be a long, short flight!

Chapter 21

Michael woke with a start and a relatively significant amount of pain. He put his hand to his head and felt the goose egg protruding out of his forehead. It was a large lump, and fortunately it wasn't going inward. He felt the caked blood on the tip of the goose egg and was happy it had stopped bleeding while he slept.

Michael looked forward. Dirt covered the cracked windshield. He remembered the gear giving way, and the nose of the plane diving into the ground. He looked to the sides and saw that the windows were still intact. The crack in the front window showed some massive spiders and one depression, but the safety glass held fast.

Michael felt his arms, legs and body. He was sore, but only his head seemed worse for the wear. He then moved his legs and they were free, which was a concern right away. Most of the plane must still be intact. Many pilots had been trapped under a yoke in a crash unable to get out.

Michael looked behind him. Some light shone through the windows and the planes interior lights dimly lit up the scene. There was no movement. Michael made his way through the door, now at an odd angle, and entered the cabin. Ziggs and his chair were against the front, the bolts having ripped loose of the floor. The man's body was contorted into a position that no artist could ever imagine. Ziggs' eyes were still open staring into a world only he could see now. Michael was unmoved, but still closed the man's eyes.

The big man was on the floor before him as well. Michael had not had time to tie him down, and he obviously had been jostled, but the man was very loose, which probably saved his life. He was alive, and Michael could only find superficial injuries. He considered him for a moment and knew that the darts were supposed to keep a man out for a dozen hours. Michael quickly tied the man's hands behind his back, knowing that he had broken similar zip ties before. He looked at the man's wrists, torn up pretty good. Price of breaking zip ties with bare skin.

Under a chair, Michael found the pilot, Zigg's cousin. He was still alive as well. He was already tied and out cold so Michael left him in his dart- induced coma.

Michael went to the aircraft door. It seemed intact but was bent in several places from impact. The door unlocked easily enough, but as he pushed it he was not rewarded with any movement. He pressed and kicked for a moment and then there was a crack of light. Straining, Michael pressed the door again and it suddenly gave way. He stepped outside into cool mountain air and surveyed the scene. They had skidded for a while into a thicket of trees. The skid would attract attention but as Michael looked, a great deal of the plane was obscured by the loose soil that they had literally burrowed into. Still, the tail and wings were mostly visible and if someone was looking, they would be found.

Michael looked around. He guessed they were somewhere in Wyoming still, but he really had little idea. The clearing was large, a few miles long, and it appeared that there was a lake at one end. The mountains were formidable, meaning he was probably around Yellowstone. This could introduce a host of problems, depending on where he was in Yellowstone, but he wasn't sure. He went back in the plane to survey his assets.

Michael found all of the bags in the back of the plane and took them outside. He took all of the weapons he could find, and anything that was not tied down, and put everything outside of the plane. He had checked the radio first, but it was shot. "Why is it the radio always falls apart?" he asked aloud.

Michael was able to find three cell phones, and though each had no signal, they might have some GPS signal. He set them aside.

The GPS in the plane was still working. A tough aviation box that would likely survive even if the plane had burnt to a crisp. Michael considered why the GPS would be so hardened and the radio would not. He filed away that he should work with some company to build a hardened aircraft radio. It seemed logical but no one really thought much about it.

Michael looked closely at the GPS, and as he had guessed, he was in the heart of Yellowstone. He widened and widened and guessed he was about 40 miles to a road, and maybe 10 miles to a ranger outpost. These outposts were not always manned, so it was likely he would be alone if he got there. It would be shelter though. He also considered the plane as shelter but was concerned about Abby and if the same group had gotten her. He needed answers, so he needed his assailant awake.

Michael found the first aid kit and looked for epinephrine. It was a risk, but he needed questions answered and knew it would help in some way. As he went through the kit, he came across Advil and Tylenol. He took 2 Tylenol and put them in his shirt pocket. He rummaged and found a case with water bottles in it. He removed one, unscrewed the lid and took a short drink. He then pulled the Tylenol from his pocket, swallowed them, and washed them down with the water. He knew he didn't need them now, but he wanted to get ahead of the aches and pains that would soon be upon him.

Michael looked at the sky and estimated he would have about 2 hours of sunlight left. He found the knife he had used on the plane earlier. He went inside and cut free Ziggs then took him outside. He covered him with the blanket that had covered Michael when his captors thought he was unconscious.

Michael then surveyed the inside of the plane. There were a variety of small predators in Yellowstone. Only black bears and cougars would really be dangerous, but it would not be good to travel at night. There were too many variables, and a person could get lost or have issues and not be able to easily recover. There were also some wolves and coyotes in the area, and they would travel in packs at night. The coyotes would be no issue, but a mid-sized pack of wolves could be a problem. Wolves usually stayed away from people, usually.

Sensibly, Michael had decided that he and the men would stay in the plane tonight, and by morning the two men would be awake. He would decide, based on their usefulness and cooperation, if he would kill them or take them with him. He had no opinion on what would be best.

Once everything was in place, Michael worked on the lights in the plane, and since the batteries were still good, got them to come back up fully. That would give them light but not heat though, so he went into the woods and collected pine needles. He then built a small pile of wood around the needles, with larger pieces around that. He was about to use the knife and make a boy scout proud when he thought again of the first aid kit. He went back to the small Urban Outfitters kit and found the matches he knew would be there. Laughing at himself, he lit a small fire and used a crisscross method to build it up. Soon the fire was raging relatively well, so he warmed himself for a moment. Michael guessed it was about 50 degrees Fahrenheit outside, and that meant night temperatures will be around freezing. He knew he had limited time to be ready.

Michael began to arrange items in the plane so they made some sense for nightfall. He tied his two ex-captors together so they would not be an issue, and he put useless items in the back. He did not want many things outside as it might attract too much animal life. He also had to do something with Ziggs, but he left that for last and would tend to him later.

Michael surveyed the weapons he had available. There was one assault rifle, a nice Palmetto Armory model. He didn't care much for it but owned one himself, and he was always impressed with the number of modifications the company made available. That and the fact that there was always its ammunition available at low prices. Michael always needed practice ammo as he only loaded his own 50BMG and other high caliber weapons.

Michael had 5 magazines with thirty shots each, and four pistols, all of them different. Fortunately, the pistols were all 9mm, of which he had about 200 extra rounds. Not enough for him, but workable. He set the weapons aside and vowed he would use some of the darkness to clean them and ensure their accuracy.

Michael looked outside. The fire he had made raged, and the area was clean, well, except for the gouged-up earth and torn up trees. It was no longer a garbage strewn mess though. Michael looked at Ziggs' body and remembered a package of garbage bags in the plane. He located them very quickly and took several outside. He then fit the blanket and Ziggs inside of them. The end result was a plastic wrapped body that might slow some scents. He carried Ziggs inside and put him in the pilot's chair and went back to the fire.

Michael looked around and saw there was some blood seepage which he knew would attract predators. Grabbing a few sticks, he went to the area and spread pine needles, lighting them on fire. He knew the scent would carry, but it would be a difficult scent to find, and the smell of fire would keep some animals at bay.

Michael then went inside and cut Ziggs' cousin free from the big man. He carried him outside and sat him up facing the fire. Taking the Epi pen, he stabbed the man in the leg and waited but nothing happened. Michael was distraught as he needed answers now. He continued to wait patiently though but still nothing, so he went in to the woods with about thirty minutes of light left. The colors of twilight were coming now. Darkness would be upon them soon. Michael got more wood and stacked it to the side of the plane. He wanted to make certain the flames burnt all night. His fuel was dumped earlier, or he would have used the fuel to keep the fire going. As it was, he had only whatever firewood he could find.

As Michael returned to the plane a second time, he noticed Ziggs' cousin on his side. Michael went over and sat the man back up and noticed his breathing had changed.

Groggy, the man asked, "What happened?"

Michael laughed. "You were stupid, and I shot you with a tranquillizer dart," he told Ziggs' cousin.

Realization dawned in the man's eyes. "You," the man said quietly to Michael.

"Yes, yes," Michael told the man. "Me, this is me, this is my arm, my leg, my ass, your face, quite a match, eh?"

"Tom?" the man asked Michael about his cousin.

"Died in the crash," Michael said. "He is behind you," he told the man. The man jumped and looked behind him.

Michael laughed. "He is not a ghost or a zombie. I wrapped up his body and put him where animals wouldn't get him. He is in the co-pilot's chair."

"He was my cousin," the man told Michael.

"I know," Michael replied and said to the man, "Before we go further, your name?"

"Bill," the man told Michael. "Bill Crank."

"I knew a Bill Crank once," Michael said. "Old guy, lived in Ivel," he told the man.

"Probably my grandpa," Bill said. "He has lived around those parts a long time." Realization dawned on Bill. "You were in Ivel?" he asked Michael.

"Yeah, for several years." Michael said. "Until some yahoos, like you guys, had to bother me. God, I wish people would just leave me alone and let me live," he said to the man.

Bill looked at Michael. "Mister, I just fly the plane. Tom got me in this for quick money. I was giving half to his daughter. She is in a bad way."

"Yeah," Michael said to Bill, "Tom told me. I know all about her, and he was not sure of who I was either. I picked on him because he was not cut out to do this. I don't think you are either. That makes you cut-rate players and I need answers."

"Yeah? "Why should I help you? You killed Tom," Bill responded to Michael.

"No, your big friend's head in the fuel dump killed Tom and almost us, but I have no problem killing you and moving on to your big friend," Michael retorted to Bill.

"Why should I believe you?" Bill asked Michael.

"Who do you think I am, Bill? What did they tell you?" Michael asked.

"They really didn't say much. Just that we were to pick you up and get you to Michigan, and we would be paid when we got there," Bill told Michael.

"So, they told you nothing about who I was?" Michael asked Bill.

"No, just to keep you out cold, and to put some clothes on you," Bill said to Michael. "That guy, Jones, was pretty clear on that. He just said you had to stay out."

Michael smiled and asked Bill, "Do you know Jones?"

"Hey, you are trying to get info from me! It ain't gonna' work," Bill told Michael.

Michael picked up a Glock 17 and fired three shots towards the woods. He then took the three pieces of brass casings and set them on the ground in a straight line next to Bill's foot. Michael looked at him and said, "Look, if you live, I need you to walk, so I am not going to put a knife in your femur like I did to Tom. Poor Tom thought I was kidding too. I left the knife there while I got dressed and then pulled it out. Here is how this is going to work for you, and trust me, I am usually far less amiable. I am going to shoot the 3 casings next to you. When I hit all three, I am going to shoot you. I think I will put the bullet right between your eyes."

The twilight was upon them and it gave the area an eerie glow that could only be from the setting or rising of the sun. Michael walked back from the man, about 25 feet. "Y'aint never gonna' hit those bullets from there!" Bill yelled. Michael turned quickly and fired one shot. The brass casing three away from the man was simply gone.

"Lucky shot," Bill said to Michael.

"Yep," Michael said, and shot a second time. The second casing was gone, and Bill stopped and looked at the two empty areas next to him.

"Okay, okay," Bill yelled at Michael. "I will tell you!"

Michael walked back to the fire and said to Bill, "Good idea."

Bill eyed the man in front of him and asked Michael, "You would have killed me?"

"And not thought a second about your death," Michael responded to Bill.

"So, what do you want to know?" Bill asked Michael.

"The girl, Abby, did they get her?" Michael asked Bill.

The man started laughing and said to Michael, "Hell no! Jones was so pissed. She killed 8 guys, her and some big guy."

Michael looked at the fire and asked Bill, "Were they going back?"

Bill looked at his silhouette in the fiery light and twilight. "I don't think so, she was gone. He said the big plane came and got her," he told Michael.

Michael smiled. "Good, Bill. You wouldn't lie to me, would you?"

"Naw," Bill said. "I saw your eyes. Grandpa looked at me that way once. Scared the crap right out of me! I knew you were serious," he told Michael.

Michael smiled at Bill and said, "A little bit."

Bill looked at Michael holding the 19 absently in his hand. "You are pretty good with that thing. Would you have been able to hit the third shot as easily?" he asked.

Michael looked at the Glock. "It is a good weapon, and yeah, I would have hit a third time. Then I would have placed a bullet in between your eyes, in perfect center."

Bill looked at Michael. "My Grandpa talked about a guy around Ivel that could shoot scary good like that. I wonder if it was you."

"Maybe," Michael said, "It just takes practice, patience and a steady hand and mind. I am glad you decided to talk, more blood would have drawn more animals."

Bill looked at him and off to the woods. He cringed a little as the night closed in upon them.

Chapter 22

Abby turned onto 28th street from the airport and saw the exit sign for I96. She got into the left lane and massaged the wheel of the car as they waited for the turn lane signal to come on. She looked next to her and saw the man in the red Avalanche truck looking at her car. She winked at the older gentleman, and he smiled. The light changed, and Abby slowly accelerated onto the ramp and then onto 96. The GPS was set a few dozen miles away, so she listened and started talking to Melody again. "So, this guy is one of only a few people Michael trusts with his weapons. If anyone knows where this tranquilizer gun was made it will be him," Abby said.

"Are you sure?" Melody asked Abby.

"Well, I am not, but it will be a good place to start," Abby told Melody. "Then we will swing to Muskegon and see what we can find."

"I have been reading a little about the area. Are you sure this lead is good?" Melody asked Abby.

"The guy died for it. Maybe we will get lucky." Abby said to Melody. "Every tick of the clock is a tick against Michael."

Melody looked serious and replied, "I understand. By the way, Abby, you know you are doing a hundred and twenty."

Abby looked down and saw what Melody did, the speedometer. "Oops," she said. She then slowed down to the Michigan speed limit of 70 and laughed. "Michael gets on me for that. He says I could never disappear in a crowd as everyone would just look for the blonde in the fast car."

"Got it," Melody responded. "Think we can eat before we

hit up everyone? I know we are in a hurry, but it would be nice to have a quick bite," she said to Abby.

"For a quick bite, are you thinking a sit down or a fast food on the way?" Abby asked Melody.

Melody thought about it. "How about a quick bite at a sit down?" she asked Abby.

Abby smiled and said to Melody, "Good answer. We are on our way to a little town outside of Grand Rapids. There has to be a bar there that has great food."

Melody smiled back at Abby and asked, "How long?"

Abby looked over and laughed at Melody. "Damn, you must be hungry. Maybe 20 minutes?"

Melody looked at Abby. "Well, if you say so," she said.

Abby laughed and told Melody, "I can make it in ten."

Melody immediately responded, "No, no, I have already experienced the Abby rocket. We can stay around the speed limit now, please. I would rather not have to explain a relative arsenal in the trunk to a police officer who is just doing his job."

"Party pooper," Abby called Melody.

The trip around the top of Grand Rapids was quick and efficient. Abby stayed with the sign marked 96 West, and she was enjoying the lack of traffic compared to most large cities. She knew that Dubois was a small town with almost no traffic, but Grand Rapids was relatively good sized and still the traffic flowed quite well. Michael had told her that this area was both beautiful and had a significant number of possibilities, but she had not been here before, only on the west coast of the state.

The GPS on her car, that Abby rarely got to drive, kept talking as she looked over the dash. The instrument cluster didn't look too difficult except it went to two hundred and twenty. The gauges were all seemingly simple with digital overlays which made the car seem both retro and modern. There would be only a few cars in this area as fast or as stylish. Michael had said there were many in the Grand Haven vicinity though when they had visited previously.

Abby sped along the highway and passed a series of trucks. She was amazed at how many pickups she saw and how few foreign cars were on the road. In other cities you would see a huge variety, and here she saw Chevy and Ford everywhere. She passed quite a few Chevy Avalanches and Ford F150s and wondered if there was a sale and said as much to Melody.

As Abby rounded a bend, there was a weird turn that merged or got off an exit. She pushed over in the DB9 and saw the first burst of traffic as 131 merged into 96. She accelerated firmly and the DB9 leapt ahead and found a way through the traffic. There were signs everywhere for historic sites and other interests the cities were older, and well established in this area. Abby was pretty sure there was a restaurant in a little town called Coopersville, and that is near where she needed to meet a gunsmith. She knew this because Jay had told her about a meeting at a bar there. He had said that they did not have any good Scotch, but they had great service, and the food was not really bar food. Jay liked to talk about bars he had been to, and in this case, he said it was "quaint but needed better liquor," to which Abby had laughed.

Abby accelerated a little as the traffic thinned out. She realized she was again creeping up in speed. She looked over at Melody and saw her pressing her imaginary brake into the floor.

"Sorry," Abby said. "It gets away from you."

Melody laughed at Abby and said, "I bet, but could you tighten the leash just a little?"

Abby laughed and told Melody, "OK."

The dark made Abby feel good. Driving at night was a favorite thing of hers to do, and driving at night in the DB9 was even more amazing. Abby looked over at Melody. "You know," she said, "this car is a feat of engineering and about the safest thing on wheels."

"More than a Subaru or Volvo?" Melody asked Abby.

"Who knows?" Abby replied to Melody. "It looks a lot better than a Subaru or a Volvo," she said as she laughed.

Melody giggled. "So how well do you know this guy?" she asked Abby.

Abby smiled. "I don't, and I didn't call ahead, but I checked, and his store is open until 8. We will stop there for a few minutes then invite him to dinner."

"You know I don't do the whole seduction thing," Melody told Abby.

Abby laughed and asked Melody, "Do you think I do?"

Melody grinned at Abby and said, "I guess not, but how will we convince him to help?"

"If I remember right, he owes Michael, so he should want to help without asking," Abby answered with a dry tone. "Otherwise, we will have to convince him," she told Melody.

Melody looked ahead as they passed an exit called, "Walker." She laughed and asked Abby, "Is the next exit, "Texas Ranger?" Both of them laughed out loud, and soon after they approached an exit for Coopersville. As they did so, they went slower and saw a sign from a huge boat dealership. "Wow!" Melody said to Abby. "They take boating seriously!"

"Michael had said that they take four things seriously up here; boating, hunting, fishing, and snowmobiling," Abby told Melody. "The rest fell into place, but those were on top. When Michael bought a weapon up here, it was always for "long range hunting" and they were good with that."

Melody looked at Abby and asked, "This isn't like a cult or a group, is it?"

Abby looked back at Melody. "No idea," she said. "I just know that Michael would rather die than let someone touch his weapons, and he lets Larry work on them. So, the guy must be trustworthy."

Melody looked over at Abby. "I get it. I'm guessing Michael has a good collection of weapons."

"You obviously don't have a lot of information on him," Abby said to Melody. "Michael has a solid collection, but only a few he is really excited about. We left a house in a hurry a few years ago and he grabbed some of the weapons, but I found he had duplicates of many at another house. You really should update your files if you are going to be watching over us."

At the Coopersville exit, Abby turned right, then almost an immediate left. A mile in, she turned right, and she and Melody were transported into a land of trains. The trains stretched for a short time, and there were passenger cars and other cars scattered through the tracks. As Abby brought the car around, she turned away from the town for a second and was greeted by a small gun store. She turned off the car and was beckoned in by a neon "Open" light.

Abby and Melody walked into the door of the store which was a lot larger on the inside than the outside. It seemed institutional, with concrete walls and floors and only a little decoration. As Melody looked around, she saw the high-tech cameras and a variety of ammunition that would make most enthusiasts proud.

"Hello there," came a voice from an older man who walked away from a computer sitting at the side. "How can I help you ladies?"

Abby looked around. There was no one else in the building at this time. "I hope you can help me. My name is Abby. Michael Masterson is my boyfriend and I need your assistance," she told the man.

"Michael who?" the man said to her while staring at her face.

"Masterson," Abby said.

The man walked closer, looked at Abby and snickered for a moment. "How is Michael?" the man asked Abby.

"Are you Larry?" Abby asked the man.

"Yeah, I'm Larry," he told Abby. "So, how is Michael?"

Abby noticed his hand was behind his back as if he was scratching a really persistent itch. "Michael is missing," she stated.

Larry kept scratching. "Missing, huh? So how do I know you

are who you say you are?" he asked Abby.

Abby looked at the man, dumbfounded, and asked, "Michael never mentioned me?"

Larry smiled and put his hands on the table then nodded towards the wall. There, on a small corkboard, was a picture of Michael and Abby holding each other. Michael had on a denim shirt while Abby, looking diminutive, was wearing a short dress. Michael held his Barret rifle at his side and Abby in his other arm. "I am just kidding with you. Bad joke, I guess. What can I do you for?" he asked Abby.

Abby looked at Melody who brought over a small box, opened it, and then brought out the tranquilizer pistol. "I was hoping you could tell me where to find whoever bought this," Abby said to Larry.

Larry looked down at the polymer weapon. It was the size of many small pistols but was sleek. It looked like a cross between a Smith and Wesson Target Pistol and one of the Ruger 22/45 pistols. He put on a pair of white cotton gloves and picked it up. It was light, heft easily. He sighted it, grabbed some glasses and looked at the sides and the magazine. "So, what does this have to do with Michael?" Larry asked Abby.

Abby unloaded a small part of the story on him. Her finding the house empty, the darts in the wall, coming to get Melody ad getting here. She left out the part where she killed a bunch of guys and was a severe badass, flying a giant plane to get to Larry. That was pretty much a need-to-know thing.

Larry was stoic as he listened, and Melody just watched. "I think you have had a bad day," he said to Abby.

Abby looked at Larry for a moment and replied, "You could

say that. I am tired, hungry, with a hungrier woman, and I am a little pissed off. I would really like your help because Michael trusts you more than pretty much any gunsmith in the world."

"Really," Larry said. "I bet I know why, but we can talk about that later. There is a restaurant named Champs around the corner. Go get something to eat and I will be over there after I make a few calls," he told Abby and Melody.

"A friend said the food there was good, but there was something else," Abby said to Larry.

"Just go eat," Larry told Abby. "I will join you and we will see what I can do for you," he said as he picked up the phone.

As Abby and Melody walked out and got in the car, they noticed the "Open" light turn off and heard a click on the door. Although it was glass, it was obvious the door had been sealed. "What do you think?" Abby asked.

"I am not sure yet," Melody answered Abby. "He was a bit guarded, but I guess he didn't know us."

Abby sat in the car and pressed the ignition button. "I know, but it is weird seeing a picture of myself on a gun store wall. I mean, I wasn't even wearing a swimsuit!" she said to Melody trying to keep a straight face. She started smiling then burst and they both laughed.

The trip to Champs was short, less than a minute, for after only one turn Abby and Melody were there. The cars lined the quaint street with an auto parts shop and a general store on the sides of the small bar and grill. From the outside it was just a door, but as they walked in, well, it was a bar. The food smelled good, and the TVs were all over the place. Conversations were rampant as the girls found a high-top table and sat down next to a jukebox.

Before Abby and Melody could even sit down, a young lady walked up and asked, "What can I get you to drink?"

Abby answered the girl, "Water."

"Wine, please," Melody told the girl.

The young lady looked at Melody and asked her, "How about a nice Michigan Cherry Riesling?"

Melody smiled and told the lady, "Sounds good, and a water too."

The girl told Abby and Melody, "The special is a prime rib sandwich and it comes with chips or fries. I will be right back with your drinks." she said and then walked away.

Abby and Melody looked around the room and noticed that there were a lot of people in the bar. Most were wearing logo wear for a variety of types of businesses. There were names of at least three tool and die shops, several auto shops, a performance auto shop, and a few farms printed on the customers' shirts.

A young man walked in with a performance auto shirt on and yelled to his buddies, "Hey, there is a DB9 out front!"

Two other young men got up, met halfway and walked outside with the first man. Melody looked at Abby and told her, "A nice Chevy Impala would have been better."

Abby smirked at Melody and said, "Bite your tongue, woman!" and Melody laughed.

The wine and water came quickly. Melody tasted the wine and went "Mmmm" in utter delight. "God, this has a nice flavor and I really needed that," she said to Abby.

Abby looked at her phone and then back at Melody.

"What's wrong?" Melody asked Abby.

"Habit," Abby told Melody. "I was going to call Michael. No phone, no number and even if he is ok, he doesn't have this number."

Melody held out her hand and grabbed Abby's arm. "We are on this. It will be okay."

"Either way it will be okay," Abby said to Melody.

The young lady came back again and asked Abby and Melody, "Decided?"

Abby ordered the special, but Melody wanted a burger, fries and onion rings. Abby looked at her and said, "Damn, where are you going to put all that?"

"I told you I was hungry," Melody told Abby.

The waitress and Abby laughed, and the girl said, "My name is Emma. I will be back in a few."

"Thanks, Emma," Abby said, and a few moments after Emma walked away Larry walked in.

"Larry!" some men yelled as the performance auto shop men followed him into the bar. "Did you see the car outside?"

Larry smiled and said to the men, "Yep, it has four wheels and moves." The men smirked at Larry as they headed back to their tables and laughed.

Larry sat down at the end of the table next to Abby and across from Melody. "I know who made the weapon. They are tracking down who it was sold to."

"Who made the weapon?" Abby asked Larry.

"Well," Larry paused for a moment, "I did," he said. "I sold several of them years ago. I have a friend searching where it ended up, but I can guess."

"Guess for me," Abby told Larry as Emma walked up.

"Hey, Larry," Emma said. "Usual?"

"Yeah," Larry said, "and a Corona this time too," he told Emma.

Emma walked away, and Abby said again to Larry, "Guess!"

"Let's wait until I know for sure," Larry said to Abby. "If I am right, well, it may be bad. If I am wrong, well, it will be hard to track."

Abby frowned and told Larry, "It is going to be bad no matter how it goes down."

Larry looked at Melody and asked, "So, what is your story?"

Melody looked Larry over and said, "Just along for the ride."

Larry laughed. "Guessing games. I would say Army, probably investigations. You keep your mouth shut too much. Probably working for some congressional group or some dipshit like Tarkington," he said to Melody. Larry looked at Abby then and said, "Yeah, I know he is your father, but he is a dipshit."

Abby smiled. "He would probably agree," she told Larry.

Melody sipped the wine, "Okay, so if I am," she said to Larry.

"Nothing," Larry said to Melody. "Just like to know what is on the table with me if I have to put my ass on the line."

Melody took another sip of wine and looked at Larry. "I get it. I am with a group with a dipshit, we clean up shit, and I am here for now but was an investigator until I was forced into this shit. Enough shit for now?"

"Good answer," Larry said to Melody and grinned a wide grin.

Abby looked at Larry and asked, "How long before we know?"

"It may be morning," Larry told Abby.

The food came surprisingly quickly. Along with their order was a grilled cheese sandwich and soup. Abby looked around and noticed a lot of people eating grilled cheese and soup and thought, "Must be good."

Larry's cell rang and he picked it up. Abby leaned forward in anticipation. "Yeah," he said. "Okay, call me first thing."

Larry hung up and looked at Abby. "Pretty sure I am right. He will verify, but it looks like you will be visiting the beautiful Lake Michigan Shoreline."

Abby looked at her food, ate a little, then sat and thought for a minute. Every moment Michael was gone was a chance he would be hurt. Someone was going to pay. Michael's voice echoed in her head saying, *"How are they going to pay if you are starving and tied up in knots?"* Abby smirked to herself and started eating in earnest. Melody was enjoying the atmosphere, and Larry just smiled and listened to the music.

Chapter 23

Alan drove to the airport. He knew many of the pilots there, but he had never tried to rent or buy a plane. His plane would not work very well in this case, mainly because it was taken apart in a hanger. He considered the distances and was hopeful there was a helicopter in the area. He had no point of reference on that though, and it was dark and would probably not be a good time to run around in the woods.

As Alan pulled into the airport, he remembered the Wings of Wyoming and drove out to their hanger. He got out of his pickup and walked around to the door, which was locked as he expected. He then walked around the hanger area and to the field facing doors and was rewarded by the sight of three men talking.

"Sorry," one of the men said to Alan. "We are closed."

Alan smiled. "Sorry for intruding. I just wanted to see if you knew anyone with a helicopter or someone with a plane, who might be willing to make a quick run," he asked the men.

"Umm, it's a little late," one of the men said. "Would morning work?" he asked Alan.

"I suppose it might have to, but I would be willing to pay someone who could swing up to the Yellowstone area really quick," Alan told the man. "I know it is late, but it is important."

"So, what's going on?" the man asked Alan.

"Sorry," Alan said to the man. "My manners. My name is Alan. I am looking for someone and I am worried they might have crashed outside of Yellowstone. I know the police and the guard will be looking, but I just wanted to make a pass myself and see if I could see them."

"Name's Tim." The man reached out and grabbed Alan's hand. Alan never meant to, but he was sometimes intimidating when he shook hands, for his hand was massively larger than most peoples'. He smiled at Tim.

"Nice to meet you, Tim," Alan said.

"I have seen you around the airport from time to time. You have the old Cessna, right?" Tim asked Alan.

Alan replied to the man, "Yeah, it is in pieces right now."

Tim laughed and told Alan, "Funny how that happens. I have a friend who owns a boat, and I used to pick at him and say he had a hole in the water to throw money into. He looked at me one day and said, "So what? You throw your money and your time in the air and expect it to come back down." We both just laughed. So, what's wrong with the Cessna? Could it be fixed?"

Alan told Tim, "It will take a bit, maybe a few weeks. I have a new fuel pump on order."

"Yeah, sometimes it is better to replace," Tim said to Alan.

A second man walked up and said to Alan, "I know you. You are the one with the dogs."

Tim suddenly had a look of recognition. "Yeah, you have those big dogs. Where are they?" he asked Alan.

"In the car. They are with me pretty much all the time. I told them to stay," Alan told the men.

"I've seen you with them. They are pretty well trained. Do that all the time?" the second man asked Alan.

Tim looked at the second man and said, "Fred, this is Alan."

Fred shook Alan's hand. He was small so his hand got lost in Alan's. He stood about 5'4 compared to Alan's 6'6, which made Alan look huge compared to him. Fred and Tim both had black coveralls on with an airplane logo that made them look like twins. Fred smiled at Alan and Alan was amazed at how white and perfect his teeth were. Fred said to Alan, "Yeah, I was with a K9 unit with the force, but your dogs are pretty well over the top. I have seen people drive by your car with dogs yapping and they don't even move. What's your secret?"

Alan told Fred, "I work with them every day." Then he asked him, "I am a little worried about my friend, so do you know anyone who would fly tonight? Better yet, know anyone that has a chopper?"

"Wish I did," Fred told Alan.

Tim answered Alan, "No idea."

Alan's phone rang. He answered, "This is Alan."

"Alan, where are you?" Alex's voice said on the phone.

"Dubois airport," Alan told Alex. "Trying to find a plane or chopper."

"Hold on," Alex said. Alan heard voices in the background and then a goodbye and a hang-up on another phone. "I found you a pilot and a chopper. It will be there in a few minutes. I had sent it to Michael's house to pick you up. You haven't been answering," Alex said to Alan.

"Sorry," Alan said. "Didn't hear the phone. I am good now. So, Yellowstone, will it have the range I need to get to where I think he went down? Do you have any more word on whether it reappeared?" he asked Alex.

"No," Alex replied to Alan. "I have two more choppers on the way, but you are closest, as of now, who has a clue as to what is going on," Alex said tersely. "I really don't want this to end up in the papers. Keep it under your hat if you can."

"A few locals know, but they will keep a lid on it," Alan told Alex. As Alan spoke the AugustaWA109 helicopter appeared and landed by the hanger near him. The blades kept turning. Alan looked at Tim and Fred and told them, "Keep this under your caps, okay? Boss's orders. Well, not my boss, but something like that. I am leaving my truck here, alright?"

"Sure," Tim said to Alan. "Your truck will be here when you get back."

Alan ran to the helicopter with his head down. He opened the door, leaned in and yelled to the pilot, "I am bringing two dogs, okay?"

The pilot gave Alan a thumb's up, so Alan blew three short whistles that probably could barely be heard over the chopper. Two black German Shepherds shot around the hanger like a bolt and were at Alan's side in seconds. Alan opened the back door and pointed, and the two dogs jumped in and lay down next to each other. Their legs were in a solidly locked position like two ebony statues.

Alan looked over at the two men he had been talking to and saw the third walk up next to them. He waved and they waved back. They all had a look of astonishment on their faces as he climbed into the front of the cockpit. Alan grabbed the headset hanging next to him and put it on, saying to the pilot, "Thanks for coming. Name's Alan, and Shiva and Vishnu are in the back." He then took out a printed map and pointing to it said, "Here is where we are going," and asking the pilot, "any issues?"

"Emerald lake?" the pilot asked Alan. "That area is pretty empty. Lots of hikers get lost up there."

"You been briefed?" Alan asked the pilot.

"Yeah, we are looking for a plane that may have gone down," the pilot replied to Alan.

Alan asked the pilot, "Enough fuel?"

"Drop tank will give us all we need. Not sure what we will find in the middle of the night," the pilot said as Alan closed up the door.

"Maybe nothing, but if the plane went down, we will find a roaring fire if someone I know lived," he told the pilot.

Alan was strapped in, and the helicopter props spun faster. The helicopter then started to lift off the ground. Alan looked behind him and saw that the two dogs were asleep on the floor of the cargo area. He was always proud of how adaptable they were, but he had worked with them well. They had been in numerous helicopters, but this one was apparently no big deal since it rode smoothly and was enclosed. Alan looked at the dash and then out the window and saw the small group waving. He waved back as they shot off to the north.

"The spot you have marked is not far, about 50 miles," the pilot told Alan. "We will be there in well under an hour. By the way, I am Karl. National Guard. We were in Dubois for a day and this call came in. Care to give me an idea of who you work for? Not often I get called out this quick with a "zero questions allowed" status."

"You may not want to know, Karl," Alan said, "When we find what we are looking for, we can ask."

Karl looked at Alan with a strange grin. "Sounds fun," he laughed, and the helicopter sped up. Alex looked down and guessed they were doing a little over 100 mph ground speed.

"How long have you been flying these?" Alan asked Karl into the headset.

Karl looked over at Alan. "Seems like forever," he said.

Alan looked back at Karl, sizing him up. He was probably 50, average height and weight, and wearing jeans and a black leather jacket. He asked him, "So, you are Guard?"

"Yeah," Karl replied to Alan. "You caught me at dinner. I was told to go in my pajamas if I needed to."

"Nice," Alan said. "Sorry, sometimes people get a little wound up," he told Karl.

"It is no issue," Karl said. "We were having meatloaf at a friend's house. I had just started eating. It was brick hard and I didn't know how I was going to do it," he shared with Alan.

Alan laughed on of his deep laughs. "Nothing like bad meatloaf," he said. "I went out with a girl once and the meatloaf she made for me was awful. I tried to give it to the dogs but they wouldn't even eat it. She caught me, gave me and the dogs a dirty look and threw us all out. I think it was for the best. My stomach wouldn't have handled dating her," he told Karl as they both laughed hard.

"Yeah," Karl said. "Meatloaf is either the best thing in the world or the terror that scares the hell out of you. My wife, well, she made the best meatloaf in the world. It is one of the reasons I married her. Damn, she could cook! Worst day of my life when she died. I think I lost weight from both my heart and my stomach that day," he told Alan.

"Sorry, Karl," Alan said. "I mean, no one likes to lose someone special."

Karl grinned. "Awkward, isn't it?" He said to Alan. "It is no issue, a few years ago. Was quick for her, cancer, but it ate her up within a month. I held her every day 'til the moment she died."

Alan smiled and told Karl, "I am sure she was a great woman."

Karl smiled. "That she was," he said to Alan. "She made the world a better place by being in it."

Alan thought about his recent times with Melody. He had only felt strongly about a few people in his life. He was around Michael occasionally and he was always amazed by his relationship with Abby. Now, he was feeling so much with Melody, even though she was younger. She seemed to just get him. It was somewhere past awesome.

"So, how do you get by day to day?" Alan asked Karl.

"Easy," Karl said. "I love to fly, and I remember her always." He opened his jacket and reached into his shirt pocket, taking out a small picture that was perfectly laminated. He handed it to Alan. It was of Karl and a striking, long-haired woman with deep dark eyes. He told Alan, "She was Cherokee, and knew how to keep me happy all the time. I worked hard to make her happy every day as well. In the end, she was the best thing that ever happened in my life."

Alan handed the picture back to Karl and said, "She was very pretty."

Karl was quiet for a second, talking into the headset on

another channel, "Alan, this is for you," he said.

"Alan, it's Alex. Wanted to make sure you are off the ground. Let me know if you need anything else," Alex said.

Alan smiled. "Having a good time up here," he told Alex.

Alex responded to Alan, "I am sure. I think Terry is going to have a stroke. Jay has been flying us upside down for about 10 minutes. He wanted to see if it was possible."

Alan laughed. "I am sure it is in those little things you fly," he said to Alex.

"Well, I am hoping we level out for a little bit. We will be touching down in a few hours in Grand Rapids," Alex informed Alan.

"I will let you know what I find up here, Alex," Alan said. "The pilot is good so we should cover a bit of area in a hurry."

"Keep me updated. The pilot can patch us in as necessary," Alex told Alan then said, "Out."

"Meat and potatoes there," Karl said to Alan.

"Tried to be an officer," Alan said to Karl.

"Happens," Karl told Alan as they sped through the night sky.

Chapter 24

"Not sure you want any part of this," Larry said. "Yeah, I will talk to you later and we will see what happens. I need to resolve it though." He hung up the phone and stared up at one of the TVs on the wall. Local news was playing, and he smiled, thought, then ran his fingers through his white beard. "Well," Larry said to Abby, "it is bad. I was worried about it, but I wasn't sure I would be right."

Abby looked at Larry unmoved. "Spill it," she said as she drank her water.

Larry looked at her and said, "There is a group outside of Muskegon. They are a little over the top. They have monthly meetings and sit around and show each other how to use guns, survive, and generally be bad people. The women are sent to the kitchen or hall to learn how to sew and cook. A lot of them live on site and I am told it is darn near slavery for some. It is a really bad group," he told Abby.

"What does that have to do with anything?" Abby asked Larry.

"Well," Larry replied, looking at Abby, "the leader of the group, Jack Jennings, is a little bit of an eccentric. He has been collecting weapons for a long time. I will not sell to him, and he doesn't like me for that. He does, however, have a lot of friends, and apparently the 5 weapons I made were sold to him indirectly," Larry said.

Abby looked down at her beer and asked Larry, "Do you know where they are?"

"I can find out," Larry answered Abby. "They have several houses in the north part of Muskegon. They are out on farms and are well protected. I will make a call, but it would take an army to get in. Most of the locations are manned with a dozen or more men."

Abby looked at Melody. "I took eight men this morning. Can you do four?"

Melody nodded her head and said to Abby, "Four, yeah, I bet I can get six, and we could make it even."

Abby took a drink. "Naw, I want a bigger stack. You can have overflow if I need it," she told Melody.

Melody looked at Abby and said, "I bet I can take eight men and you will have to take four."

"Enough!" Larry said to Abby and Melody, loud enough that several people turned and looked at him. He shrunk a little and whispered then, "This isn't a game. These people are well trained and serious."

Abby looked at Larry, her blue eyes shining like crystal beacons. "You think I am kidding? This isn't a game. I took eight men this morning and did it with no compunctions. If it means getting Michael back, I will take fifty more to their graves and dance on them along the way. All I can say is they fucked with the wrong girl."

Melody looked at Larry and told him, "Backup is coming so we are covered and then some."

Larry shook his head. "Leave it to Michael to have a girlfriend like you, Abby."

Abby smiled, then set the half bottle of beer aside and began drinking water. "Can you get me an address?" she asked Larry.

Larry said, "Be right back." He walked outside, and Abby looked at Melody. "This is my fight, you don't have to go. I don't want you getting hurt on my account."

Melody looked back at Abby. "And miss this chance to see the real Abby in action? Everyone says Tarkington is the 'General of Gore.' Looks like he has a 'Deadly Daughter'."

Abby smiled and asked Melody, "Any idea where the group is? I really don't want them to interfere."

"You know, they can help, and we could do this together," Melody told Abby.

"They could, but this is my problem and I want someone's head for what they did to Michael," Abby said forcefully to Melody.

Chapter 25

Michael put more wood on the fire and worked the coals. It was a good blaze, and he knew it would keep most animals at bay. His sleeping beauty had now woken but was still groggy as he looked back and forth at Michael and the wilderness.

When he had been awake a few minutes, Michael drug the man outside. It was now Michael, Bill and this man watching the fire.

"What's your name?" Michael asked the man.

"His name is Greg," Bill told Michael.

Michael looked at Bill and said, "Well, that's nice, but maybe Greg needs to answer."

"Oh," Bill said to Michael. "Sorry."

Michael looked back at Greg. "What's your last name, Greg?"

Greg eyed Michael with razor anger. "None ya'."

Michael looked at Bill and said, "You know, I don't think Greg here likes me."

"Greg didn't seem to like anybody," Bill said to Michael.

"Shut the fuck up, hillbilly!" Greg yelled at Bill.

"It is just a matter of time, boy." Greg said to Bill. "I am gonna' get out, and when I do, I am gonna' fuck you up!"

Michael laughed. "God, I have heard that joke a lot of times. So, Greg, did the powers that be tell you who I am, or are you as clueless as Bill here?"

"You are a job, faggot!" Greg hissed at Michael. "Nothing more, nothing less. You'll pay the bills and keep my women up. There ain't no use of you knowing me or me knowing you. You are meat, and I am gonna' cook you!"

Michael started giggling, got up and danced around the fire. "I am meat, and I am gonna' get cooked!" Michael yelled in a deep voice.

"Yeah, keep yelling, you dumb mother fucker!" Greg spat at Michael. "This is gonna' be over soon!"

Michael smiled and looked at Bill. "Should I let him go and see if he has what it takes?" Bill shook his head no. "Should I just kill him?" Michael asked with a bit of sarcasm.

"You ain't got the guts," Greg told Michael. "They send us out to catch you wannabes and you just don't get it. None of you are competition, none of you can hold a candle to us. I should have killed your ass when we put you in the plane. No, that isn't what that dumb shit wanted. He just wanted another one of you."

Michael smiled and said to Greg, "Oh, they want me?"

Greg spit on the ground. "Fuck, I doubt they know you," he told Michael. "They just want someone who is good. You fuckers aren't good. Can't even shoot that gun I bet, dumb faggot."

"I can assure you I am not a faggot for I have a girlfriend. I am not sure who you think I am, but let's see," Michael said, laughing at Greg. He drew the weapon quickly and fired twice. Bill cringed as he looked. Michael laughed some more.

Greg was wide-eyed for a second. "See, you dumb shit, you

missed! You can't even hit me from there," he yelled at Michael.

Bill looked at Greg, telling him, "Dude, he shot your ears off!"

Greg swung his head a little and blood landed on the ground in front of him. "What the fuck did you do, faggot?" he yelled at Michael. You took my ears!" Somewhere between the words and the feel of the blood running down his face, realization hit. "Who the fuck are you?" Greg screamed, as his demeanor changed.

"Who are you, Greg?" Michael asked.

"I ain't saying nothing," Greg answered Michael.

Michael laughed. "I could do dumb things and throw rocks or be stupid with you, but now I know you know more than poor Bill here. His cousin knew nothing. You Greg, you know something. I think you should tell me what it is."

Greg looked at Bill. "What did you tell him?"

"I am smart. I told him the truth," Bill said to Greg. Then they all heard it at once. Michael stood and saw that there was a helicopter in the distance heading their way. He then took another few pieces of wood and threw them on the fire. The pine caught quickly and the fire burned more brightly. In a moment, the helicopter was over them and the AW109 landed about 100 feet away from the fire. Alan emerged from the side of the helicopter and slid the back door open then ran to the fire.

"Damn, Alan," Michael said.

Alan looked at Michael. "What?"

"You couldn't wait five minutes so this guy could tell me

who tried to kill me?" Michael asked Alan.

"Do you want me to go back up?" Alan asked Michael.

"No, I need him to tell me who tried to kidnap me," Michael told Alan.

"Fuck you both!" Greg yelled at Michael and Alan. "Arrest me, you dumb shits!"

Alan looked down and told Greg, "I'm not the cops."

Michael looked at Greg. "Wanna' tell me, or tell Shiva?"

Alan looked at Michael. "Really, you would make Shiva so happy if you let them do it!" The rotors of the helicopter slowed and the sound kept going down.

"I am not telling you or Shiva a damn thing!" Greg told Michael.

Alan looked at Michael and whistled a short tone three times. The two massive dogs jumped out of the now silent helicopter and ran at full speed to Alan. They ignored everything and stopped in front of him, sitting at attention.

"Last chance," Michael said to Greg.

"They ripped one of his guys in half this morning," Alan told Michael. "The guys tried to get Abby. It was a bloodbath."

"Is Abby okay?" Michael asked Alan.

"Yeah, she is fine. She is on her way to Michigan to find you," Alan told Michael.

"Do you have a phone that works," Michael asked

"Won't matter, they were tracking her phone, she is off grid," Alan replied.

The dogs did not move and waited patiently. Their eyes never left Alan, but anyone could see they were watching the whole area. As they sat, their ears rotated for every sound made while the two men talked.

Alan walked to the pile of firewood Michael had left. He picked up a piece about two inches thick, walked over to Greg, put it next to his wrist and then walked back to Michael.

"What the fuck?" Greg said out loud.

"Shh," Michael said to Greg. "You will like this."

Alan said, "Shiva," and the dog stepped forward. Alan threw the wood in the air and Shiva caught it easily, dead center. Alan looked at the beautiful black German Shepherd and made a pinch with his fingers. The wood began creaking in the dog's mouth. Alan closed his fingers and the wood literally screamed until it splintered completely and snapped in half. Shiva pushed its tongue in and out, clearing the splinters, then looked at Alan.

Alan smiled and said, "Shiva," and the dog stepped forward again. Alan pointed at Greg's leg, and the dog trotted over and, with no effort, picked up his leg by the ankle. Greg tried to kick Shiva, but the dog pulled back. "Vishnu," Alan said, and the second dog walked to him. He pointed at Greg's other leg. Vishnu grabbed the man by that ankle in a swipe as he tried to kick. It was pinned solid. Greg tried to struggle but his arms were tied fast with cable ties, and his legs were held by two giant masses of sinew and bone.

Alan made his fingers in a pinch symbol and Greg started screaming. "I know you! I know who you are!" he yelled at Alan. "Stop, stop, STOP! I will tell you!"

Alan moved his hand out and pointed to the ground next to him. The dogs dropped Greg's legs without a thought and were at Alan's side in an instant.

Michael grinned. "Wow, he knows you," he said to Alan, "but he doesn't know me?"

"So, talk," Alan told Greg and looked at Michael, "I doubt he really knows me."

Greg looked at Alan. "You really the Silent Wolf?"

Alan laughed and said, "He does know me."

Michael looked upset and said to Alan, "I feel hurt."

Alan smiled. "I bet he knows your call sign," Alan told Michael. "Service, right?" he asked Greg.

Greg looked at Alan. "Yeah, worked for the feds for a while, and then went to Iraq."

Alan looked at Michael then Greg. "You know the Bastard Son?"

Greg laughed. "A kid's story to scare little army boys into playing nice."

"Hear that Michael? You are a kid's story," Alan said with a grin.

Michael looked down at Greg. "What is the story?"

Greg spilled, in a major way. He too was hired a short time ago and had worked to capture several people. It was a small job, but none of the men put up much fight. He told them about rumors and about the targets being taken to Michigan but really didn't

169

know where. He knew it was said to be major, but there had never been a snag until now.

Michael looked at Alan and grimaced. "Time to go."

"What about us?" Greg asked Michael.

"We will send someone back for you in a few," Michael told Greg.

Alan limped back to the helicopter. "What's wrong with you?" Michael asked.

"Got shot for you," Alan replied to Michael.

"And here I didn't get you a present," Michael told Alan.

The dogs and Michael jumped into the back of the helicopter and Alan got in the front. The doors closed, and it was Alan who said, "Can we make it to Salt Lake?"

Bill and Greg watched the helicopter take off and rocket to the south while still tied to their seats. The fire blazed as the helicopter disappeared in the distant sky.

Chapter 26

The G650 glided to a landing. It did not power a landing, nor did it force a landing. The plane nosed up and rode the wind into the Grand Rapids Airport without a transition. The plane was in the air one moment, then on the ground, no jump or bump while the speed was slow enough that the brakes were only tapped.

Terry had given up trying to understand the pilot of his plane, and he breathed a sigh of relief as the plane hit ground. There were cheers from the cabin, and Terry thought he knew how they felt as the ride had been a series of aerial acrobatics, he had not known the 650 would do. The plane had held to his surprise, but he was sure the crew was well past irritated with the hijinks of the pilot.

As the plane came to a stop outside of the hanger and next to the far larger Happy Scotsman, the Terry exited the cockpit to cheers and Jim saying, "Most fun we have had up here in a while."

"I had to see what this thing would do," Jay said as he laughed one of his huge belly laughs.

Terry frowned and said to Jim, "This maniac could have gotten us killed."

Jim laughed and told Terry, "We could be killed just about every ten minutes. Might as well have fun doing it."

Jay giggled and bowed to the group. "By the way, I wouldn't kill you," he told Terry.

Terry was still frowning and said to Jay, "Sure, I am betting you could have slipped and killed us all."

"I'm betting you could have slipped and bored everyone to

death," Jay said to Terry.

"Fuck you!" Terry, getting angry, said to Jay.

Jay raised an eyebrow. "Look boy, you want to attack my flying, fine. You want to say you hate my plane, fine. You make it personal, well, we can go outside, and I have no issue showing you mine if you want to whip out yours," he told Terry.

Terry looked confused. Jim and Rachel stared at them both, looking at one then the other. Terry then stared at Jay, looking like he was going to explode. Jay looked at Terry, coldly, impassive with a smile on his face that would scare the Cheshire cat. The tension was so thick you could cut it with a knife. Even Alex was quiet and looking at the two men. Jay and Terry took a step forward, hugged and started laughing hard.

"Did I miss something?" Rachel asked Jim.

Jim laughed and said to Rachel, "We both did."

Jay and Terry looked at the group. "We were fucking with you," Jay told them.

Terry started laughing. "I wanted to see how far we could take it."

Ronnie spoke up. "That wasn't very nice."

Barbara grimaced. "Terry, you asshole! I know you wouldn't get mad about this, but you had me fooled." She looked at the group. "We have done loops in this thing out playing around. He is such a jerk."

Alex looked at them all. "Guys, we are on the clock. It is time to hit the road and head to wherever."

Jim looked at Alex. "What is wherever?"

Jay picked up his phone. "I guess I need to call Abby on the burn phone."

Alex told Jay, "See if they have leads."

Jay grinned and replied to Alex, "I think I know how to do this."

The rest of the group began unloading the plane and moments later two big Suburbans showed up to the hanger. Jim laughed. "Nothing says government nutcase like a black Suburban."

Rachel punched Jim in the shoulder and said, "At least I won't have to lean on you."

Jim looked at Rachel and told her, "You like leaning on me. At least you do when you are snoring and drooling."

Jay was at the back of the plane on his phone. "Abby, you can't do this alone. We will be there later, within a few hours. Can't you wait for us?" he asked her. Jay nodded his head and everyone watched him as they worked. "I am sure it can wait until morning."

Alex looked at Jim and asked, "This can wait 'til morning?"

"Maybe," Jim replied, "but I wouldn't count on it."

"I think we should go now and storm whatever she has found," Rachel said.

"Of course, you do," Jim said to Rachel. "You are more aggressive than I am now."

"Of course, I am," Rachel said. "I will push into the enemy since it makes them defend. I am not going to wait for them to come to me. Besides, if they have Michael and haven't killed him, well, time is not on our side."

Jim nodded. "But we don't want to go walking into an enemy's place in the middle of the night. It would be suicide," he told Rachel.

Rachel paced a little. "What, we are here, so what if it is night? Every one of us has walked into hell in the middle of the night. It is no issue," she told Jim.

Jay walked over to Jim and Rachel. "Okay, Abby knows who got the dart guns, and that apparently is who has or may have Michael. They are on the north side of Muskegon, but some guy is trying to track down where. We have no good information right now except North Muskegon, Michigan. We should clean up, get settled and get some food, then jump to it when we know more."

Alex looked at Jay then told the group, "We should clean up, get settled and get some food, then jump to it when we know more. Everyone pack up the cars. Let's be out of here in 10. I am sure there is a place to stay and eat in Muskegon. We will be closer and will jump on it as soon as we have a target."

Rachel looked downtrodden. Jim smiled. Ronnie was red because Barbara held his arm tightly. Then Rachel was livid. "Let's see how we can push it and find a way to solve this before 24 hours goes by!" she stated. "We need to end this now!"

Alex looked at Rachel, walked closer and leaned up to her ear. "Stand down," he whispered very quietly.

Rachel looked down, looked back up at Alex, then looked down again. "Yes, sir," she said.

Alex was more forceful. "Load up. Do it now!" he told the

group.

The team scurried and got to the trucks. Jay, Jim, Rachel, and Jay took the front truck, and Terry, Barbara and Ronnie took the second one.

The guards changed shifts quickly and the planes were secured by National Guard soldiers.

Alex smiled as Jim put the Suburban in gear and dropped off towards the exit with Terry in close pursuit. The gates opened and the two trucks headed out to the freeway, following the path Abby had taken only a few hours ago.

Chapter 27

Abby was restless. Larry had told her to wait until morning. He said that he had addresses but needed to verify them. He also told her that he shouldn't have her coming in waving guns and killing people. He said that it would be dawn and he would give her everything she needed.

Abby was sitting where there was a lakeside view from the Shoreline Inn in downtown Muskegon. The hotel stood out like a gleaming pillar against all the other areas in the city. She waited impatiently then got up and walked to the balcony again, looking out over the dark lake. She saw the green lights in the center, the shining light of a tower, and multiple lights on the further shore.

Kentucky had lakes, but even the larger lakes were smaller than most of the small lakes in Michigan. It seemed every few moments there was water, and the people in the area reveled in it. They went fishing and boating, and they participated in a plethora of water sports. Now they slept in their beds, the citizens of Muskegon, while someone was potentially hurting Michael. Abby could not sleep, nor could she dream of the fantastic nights she and Michael had together. She could only think of him as he might be right now.

Melody looked at Abby staring out at the water. "You know, worrying will not make it better. It will only make you muddled."

"What did you say?" Abby asked Melody.

"I said simply, worrying will not make it better, it will keep you from being your best," Melody repeated to Abby. "We will be there as soon as Larry gets here or calls, but we can do it together. I sure haven't done anything important but listen."

Abby turned and looked at Melody, "You're right."

Melody looked at her. "Gee thanks, Abby. Now I really feel like a fifth wheel."

Abby smiled at Melody. "Not about that, about worrying. Michael always said he didn't think about it, he did it. That worrying about the target or tomorrow only kept him from being his best. He was funny. He told me a story about a show he watched on a rerun when he was a kid called Star Trek. Have you watched it before?"

"Of course," Melody said to Abby. "Why?"

"Michael said there was one show, I think he said Babel something," Abby started to tell Melody.

"Journey to Babel," Melody told Abby.

"That's it," Abby said. "Michael said the ship in there was the key to life. I now understand how he feels sometimes. I mean, I always did a little, but I am so keyed up I am in knots. I really just need to let it go and operate at 150%," she told Melody.

"I am not sure I follow you," Melody said to Abby.

"Easy," Abby continued. "In the show the ship was little and beating the Enterprise, not because it was always stronger, but because it was never planning on coming back," she told Melody.

"Yeah, I remember," Melody responded to Abby.

"Michael said if you think about the outcome constantly, you will lose sight of the moment, and the battle is won by winning moments," Abby said to Melody.

"Makes sense," Melody said. "What does that have to do with you?" she asked Abby.

"I need to let go and not worry about Michael or about

tomorrow. I need to get some sleep, find my way, and tomorrow I need to be more than I could ever be predicted to be," Abby said.

Melody smiled at Abby. "So that makes it better?"

Abby laughed. "Well, I think it makes sense now. I just need to slide away from it all and slip into sleep. I can be ready then," she said to Melody.

Melody looked at Abby. "Is it really that easy?"

Abby looked back at Melody and said, "I think it'll be. I can make it work. Michael is the best, but he does not define me. I define me."

Melody smiled. "Sounds good," she said to Abby.

Abby grinned then walked to one of the queen beds. "Good night, Melody."

Melody sat on the other bed in Victoria's Secret pajamas and put her laptop on her legs. The black slacks and pink top made her look younger than she was. She fired up her laptop and logged on to the wireless, making sure to secure the connection. She got an email right away from Alan that said, "Going to check on a crash site. Could be safe. Dogs and I are good. Missing you by the moment. Alan."

Melody smiled at the email, wondering how Alan was. They had been together only a small time, but it seemed like forever. He was older, but when she held him, it seemed like her world was complete, never having been as much as it could be. "Abby, I got an..." Melody started, but as she looked over, Abby was already in a deep sleep. She decided she needed to sleep as well. She put the computer on the table, and as it closed down, she didn't notice the new message icon. Moments later the screen was black, and

Melody was fast asleep as well.

Chapter 28

Larry paced back and forth waiting for a call. He had sent the girls to the Shoreline Inn in Muskegon to shield them just in case. As he paced, he absently spun a 45 cartridge in his fingers. He was normally calm, but he really didn't want to get back in the middle with either Jack or Michael.

Michael was one of Larry's best customers. The custom shells for the high-end sniper rifles Michael used were easy to find, but the loads he wanted were precise. Larry had made good money working with Michael to ensure he had the best ammunition available. It wasn't until later that Larry asked about what Michael was doing with those shells. He had assumed it was competition shooting, but when Michael told him the truth about working for the government, and working for private groups to eliminate targets, Larry did not want to be involved. Michael had respected that and told him it was okay.

Larry had asked Michael years later why he told him, and Michael simply said, "Why lie? The truth works even if it is unpleasant." This started an uneasy but positive relationship with Michael, but still Larry did not want to lose all he had for anyone. He had a wife to take care of as well.

Jack was an entirely different issue. Larry had never been able to put a finger on it when he was younger, but he now believed all the legends of the Michigan Militia had started with the group Jack worked with. They were tenacious and powerful and pressed the envelope daily to try to make their agenda, "the" agenda. Larry had steered clear, and if they bought from him, it was off the shelf only. Jack knew that he could not cross a line with Larry, and vice versa. As such, they had a very simple balance. It was built of mutual exclusion and a lack of real trust, but a tentative trust built on who knew more about the other.

Larry continued pacing, the 45cartridge in his hand, warm with his body heat. It seemed to have a life of its own as he spun it over and over in his hand.

His phone rang. "Hello," Larry answered.

"Are you getting involved after all these years?" a voice came.

"Jack?" Larry asked.

"Yes, it is Jack. I heard you had some visitors. You should have let me know they asked about me," he told Larry.

"Who said they asked about you?" Larry asked Jack.

"Do you think you are the only one who is in that wasted bar? C'mon, Larry. I have eyes and ears all over," Jack said. "What did you tell them?"

"Not much to tell, is there? Just that you may have been in the middle, and you have my weapons," Larry stated to Jack.

"I knew using those guns was probably too much, but the risk was worth it. In fact, they performed flawlessly, and you should be proud. I would apologize for having to get them through a secondary source, but I knew you would never sell them to me," Jack responded to Larry.

Larry turned slightly red and fired back at Jack on the phone. "Because I knew if you had them, you would do something stupid with them! Do you have any idea who you are messing with?"

"Of course, I would use them or have them used. Why have something as amazing as those little pistols just to have them?" Jack asked Larry. "I also know exactly who your pet is. I have access to a lot of files through some sources. Though most of them are blacked out, well, I just had to meet this person who stopped coming to you, over principal."

"So obviously you don't know what you have done, or who will come. You don't care except for your little group," Larry said. "How long do you think you can hide out in the little complex up by Double K? They will dig you right out and string you up like it was the 1800s," he told Jack.

"How melodramatic," Jack said of Larry. "Do you think I care if they come? I can hold off an army if I need to. Right now though, I really need to deal with you."

Larry looked at the door as the glass started to display pockmarks from weapon hits. He ducked behind the counter and grabbed the 12gauge shotgun there. Peaking up, he saw the glass broken and a small hole was apparent. Moments later, a grenade came bouncing through the hole and hit the floor. It rolled towards him, so Larry ran to the second set of counters and dived behind them as the grenade exploded. The counter fell over on him, and he groaned in pain.

He heard the voice on the phone. "Thanks Larry. Nice talking to you," Jack said.

The car outside screeched away. Larry pushed on the counter that was on top of him, but it did not move. He strained and slowly worked himself free from underneath it. He did not appear to be bleeding, so he scooted forward, then shimmied on the floor to his phone. The screen was blank. He slid the face and unlocked it, and then he dialed the number he had for Abby.

Larry's store was right next to the Sheriff's station, so he knew they would be here in moments. He wondered how Jack would have taken that chance. He figured that he must have been doing something to get the police and Sherriff out of the area while he had been talking to him. Larry cursed himself. It was an amateur mistake.

The phone rang. "Hello?" a groggy voice said.

"Abby," Larry asked, "is that you?"

"This is Melody," the voice returned. "Abby is asleep," she told Larry.

"Double K Ranch, just to the east of it, that's where you will find the buyer of the weapons. His name is Jack Jennings. Jack will be ready. He will be ready for an army," Larry told Melody then hung up the phone.

Larry heard the men throwing aside the door and walking in. "Larry, you okay?"

"I think so," he told the men.

"Larry, you are bleeding," one man said.

Larry looked down and saw the small pool of blood. His eyes crossed for a moment, dizziness overcame him, and then it got dark. He was out.

Chapter 29

The Quality Inn was not the Ritz, but it was livable. The interior of the hotel had obviously gone through several iterations as it matured. The rooms facing the pool were dated but still nice inside. Alex sat in one of the lounge chairs outside the rooms, looking at the now silent pool area. It had closed an hour ago, but the chairs and tables were still available. The business area had a significant amount of commerce, including cheap fast food and a few sit-down restaurants. Alex was happy they had found a place to stay, but they needed to eat as well and slow down a little. It was late, very late, and as he looked around, he saw that his choices were limited. It looked like a night of fast food for him.

Alex was considering their next move when Jim came out of his room and walked over to him. "Any chance we are going out together to eat something?"

"Not many choices," Alex told Jim.

"Then how about we run and grab a few dozen burgers before Rachel eats Ronnie or something similar?" Jim asked Alex.

Alex smiled and said to Jim, "Good idea. Let's ask what everyone wants for fast food and just go grab some."

Jim laughed. "Not a big choice. In cases like this where there are seven of us, and one of us could eat more than the other six, we should just get 24 burgers and leave it at that," he told Alex.

"Sure, Jim." Alex said. "Let's do that."

Alex walked toward the door and Jim followed. "I'll go with you."

"I thought you would," Alex said to Jim. They walked outside to the literal quiet compared to DC or even Richmond. The sounds they heard were few and far between. Businesses lined up like silent sentinels waiting for dawn to come alive again. Even those huge national chains that were always open sat dark and waiting for tomorrow.

As they reached a Suburban and got in, Jim spoke to Alex. "You know, you are doing the right thing."

Alex looked at Jim. "Getting burgers?"

Jim smiled. "No, you dip, by being here. It looks like you are questioning everything," he said to Alex.

Alex looked out the window as he started the car. "I know, it is just as before. I feel a little out of control," he told Jim.

Jim smiled. "Alex, you remember that movie, "Instinct"? Remember the lesson, we are all truly out of control?"

Alex looked at Jim as he made the turn to the fast-food areas. "Jim, I know it is a universal truth that we have no control of a lot of stuff, but you and I and the team are different. We are usually in control. These issues with Masterson, there are larger forces playing and we have partial information. It means we can barely control ourselves. I know Tarkington used Masterson to solve bigger or more complicated issues, but some of these things are nuts. We have no idea what we are walking into, and there doesn't seem to be a single file we can get to that isn't a series of dead ends. We also don't know if this is from something he did with us, someone else, or some nightmare that is random."

Jim looked at Alex. "So what. You have a team that is ready to follow you to the gates of hell. You just have to make sure you are opening the door and showing them where to go."

Alex pulled into a drive-through and waited behind half a dozen cars. "Jim, I don't want to lose anyone else. I mean, Lisa, well, I am sorry."

Jim looked at the dash for a moment. "Alex, listen and listen good." He paused, choked a little, fought back a tear then said, "I am saying this not as a report, but as your friend. Lisa was a good member of the team. She put herself out there, she knew the risk, and that was it, she was done. Stop making her death a fallacy for us all. Make it what it is, something that happened, and you protected the team. Should I say 'what about Mark?' How did you like them apples? Mark's dead. He would have followed you beyond hell, maybe even to do a little rectal work on Satan himself, and here you are whining about one team member. It was you that pushed words down my throat for so long, 'one person does not a team make'. Are you a liar?"

Alex looked at the steering wheel and replied to Jim, "I know, but..."

Jim broke in before Alex could finish. "No buts. Let's get this job done. Damnit, look at the odds we have overcome and come out on top! The team just keeps getting better. Stop making it worse."

Alex turned and looked at Jim. "I take that into consideration each day."

"Alex, I know you do. You don't waiver, don't show weakness. Next time just say you are going out to get a bag full of burgers, and don't ask for opinions. You and I both know, when the chips are down, it is no time to consider the moments as collaboration time. You need to decide and make it right."

Alex was quiet as he pulled up to the drive through. "Can I take your order please?" said a voice from the box. Alex looked at

Jim then said, "Give me 16 cheeseburgers and 8 hamburgers and 7 large fries."

The box cackled. "Anything else?" the voice asked Alex.

Then came a quick answer. "No," Alex replied to the voice.

Jim smiled at Alex and said, "See, I am good to have around, not only for the comic relief, but I can show a little enlightenment sometimes."

"Jim," Alex said. "I am sorry about Lisa."

Jim looked out the window. "You know, I got to know Lisa, only to lose her. I spent time with her, only to see more time taken away. We shared a lot of great things in common, but I will be able to let her go. Sure, she will still be in my head, but she won't make me miss a day, because I enjoyed every moment I had with her," he told Alex.

Alex sighed and said to Jim, "That's why I am sorry."

Jim was terse for a moment. "Again, stop it! Yes, Lisa was special, but so is everyone on the team. Yes, she opened my eyes to what I should be, but so what? You need to focus on us as a team. Damnit, Alex, Lisa is dead! She is worm food! She will not be coming back, not even in a bad zombie movie! She is just gone."

Alex looked stunned but listened to Jim.

Jim continued. "Lisa opened my eyes and let me trust, and someday I will trust again. She opened a lot of eyes. She opened Michael a little to me, and she was strong and firm and lived for the moment. Am I sad? Yes. I am happy too though, because I got to spend time with her. Do you get me?"

The car moved up to the window and Alex paid for the five sacks full of food. "Did you need any drinks, sir?" the clerk asked.

Jim leaned over and asked the clerk, "Got Kentucky Bourbon?"

"No, sir," the clerk told Jim.

Alex smiled at the clerk and said, "We are good." Jim laughed and Alex paid the bill quickly and drove off. He looked at the short distance to the hotel and wished he had longer to talk to his long-time friend. "Thanks, Jim."

Jim smiled and asked Alex, "Remember what Tarkington said to you a long time ago?"

Alex laughed and told Jim, "Yes, I know where my balls are." The two men got out of the car and walked to the door. They walked in and saw the team sitting at the table playing poker. Alex walked in with bags while Jim carried one behind him.

"Best I can do, guys. Dig in," Alex told the group.

Jim looked at them all and said, "But the fries are mine."

Rachel got up and challenged Jim. "Yeah, little man, we will have to go at it if you want all the fries."

Jay grabbed the fry bag quickly from Jim and said, "These are mine!"

Jim was just as quick and grabbed the fry bag back from Jay.

Alex turned. He knew others in the hotel were facing the area and did not want to wake anyone. He looked at Jim and said, "Spread out the fries, now!"

Jim looked at Alex, smiled and said, "Yes, sir!"

The crew ate together quietly. A few of them were playing poker for fries now and trying to wind down from a very long day.

Chapter 30

Abby woke with a start. Melody was getting dressed after she obviously had taken a shower. She looked over at Abby. "Feel better?"

Abby looked back at Melody and answered, "Yes, I feel good. Did we hear back from Larry?"

Melody turned on the news. A man was explaining how there was an attack on a gun store outside of Grand Rapids. He gave details and showed Larry limping out of the store. There was smoke and glass everywhere in the pictures and it made Abby mad. "When did this happen?" Abby asked.

"About an hour ago, right after Larry called. I got in the shower and got ready. I was about to call Alex," Melody told Abby.

Abby looked at Melody. "Larry called and you didn't wake me?"

Melody frowned. "We are about to be up against an army. Larry said even an army couldn't take them on. I was waiting for Alex," she told Abby.

Abby looked at the TV and the damage. "Let's get a move on. Where are they, what time is it?" she asked Melody.

Melody looked at Abby and turned her computer towards her. "It is 6:00 am. It is a little place just to the north of here. It is around the Double K ranch, but it is walled off and looks like a game hunting area. Tall fences and lots of security. I looked at satellite and it looks like a big training area. ATF has tried to get in several times, but the group is connected. Everything stops before it gets started, which means someone else is likely involved. I did a little digging in our databases."

Melody touched a screen and the picture changed. "It looks like this man, Jack Jennings, is in charge." A picture of a short man with a wide chest and big arms, working with a group of other people, came up. "He skirts the law. Last count by ATF there may be 100 people involved, and the estimate could be as high as 1,500."

"So, what do they do?" Abby asked Melody.

"Likely sit around and train, and it looks like they train a lot," Melody answered Abby. "Over fifty thousand rounds of ammo have gone out in the last year. ATF has tracked the orders that they know of to get that number. This area has a lot of outdoor clubs. Hell, I saw a notice that schools are closed for deer season. It is a different world."

"Not so different," Abby said to Melody with a smile. "Just another location."

"What do you mean?" Melody asked Abby.

"C'mon, Melody. There are undergrounds everywhere, places where people meet and are a little off the beaten path. Everyone thinks it is just in the hills and the rural areas, but it is just as bad in the city. The weekend warriors who think they are experts. The militias that protect their neighborhoods from whatever they have thought up. The hoodlums that think they are being tough and instead just perpetuate the hoodlum ideas from the past. It is not different; it is just more visible. Hard to see the crazies in a city filled with people. Michael laughed about it once with a guy in Kentucky. They called it 'security by obscurity'. The neighbor is not noticed because there are too many neighbors to notice," Abby said.

Melody sat for a moment. "You are probably right, Abby. I would always find more trouble in the city, but it was always well hidden."

Abby grinned. "In the country, you can see trouble coming and resolve it. Michael and I try to keep the locals at arm's length but happy with us. There is an uneasy peace, and sometimes an easy peace. In Ivel, it is likely no one would have easily gotten to us until Alex and 7 others showed up. That house had too many eyes on it. The locals liked us," she told Melody.

Melody asked Abby, "How did they find you?"

Abby looked down. "Michael has an aunt who tries to help everyone, and she let someone know where Michael was," she told Melody. "It was all a trap to try to kill Michael though, so he did the only smart thing."

"What was that?" Melody asked Abby as she cocked her head.

"Michael blew up the house," Abby told Melody and laughed. "I am going to shower and get dressed while you finish, but we are going with or without your group."

Melody picked up her phone and dialed Alex.

"Hello," Alex said after only one ring.

"It's Melody," she said to Alex.

"I have caller ID," Alex told Melody.

"I am well aware of that," Melody said to Alex. "But anymore, who knows who is calling? Anyway, Abby is going after this guy, with or without you."

"Going after who?" Alex said quickly to Melody.

"The man's name is Jack Jennings," Melody started, "and he is a resident up here. He also seems to have a little area set aside to hunt game, train domestic terrorists, and get special weaponry from exotic dealers. He is listed with the ATF and is on the FBI watch list. He is well protected by local government. Most of what he does seems to be well under the radar, and Abby may be walking into an army of anywhere from 100 to 1,500 men to try to get Michael back."

"Not really liking those odds. Any way we can find out more for sure?" Alex asked Melody.

Melody paused then answered Alex. "I can try to see if there have been any heat signatures, but who knows? The one area could be masked by dozens of others. There is a lot of space up here, and with space there are capabilities of spreading things out. There is also a lot of water up here, and well, it can keep hot things cool pretty easily."

Alex then asked Melody, "What about records of money?"

"I already dug into that, and the records are pretty thin. If you read them as they are written, well, they operate on zero budget as a deer game farm. It costs about three hundred dollars a year and they make five hundred dollars a year. A nice margin, but pretty silly if you think about it," Melody answered Alex. "I was curious why they have never been audited. Well, it's simple. It is listed as a non-profit."

Alex sighed on the phone. "So, do we know anything?" he asked Melody.

"Not really," Melody said. "I have no idea why anyone would take Michael to this place. I can't find a connection between the two. I can't see any correlation between this area and Michael or anyone else, except for an obscure land purchase on Lake Michigan. Even that is so well hidden I am sure no one will easily find it," she told Alex.

"How did you find it?" Alex asked Melody.

"Accident," Melody told Alex. "I was searching Masterson and got a side hit, but it was in a Mikey Masterson name with all the necessary paperwork and was paid in cash. It was the cash transaction that got me looking further."

"Why?" Alex pressed Melody.

"It was five hundred thousand dollars and none of the correct forms were filled out. Just a few obscure land transfer documents. It didn't match up," Melody replied to Alex.

"Okay, send me directions. We'll head out now and beat Abby there," Alex said to Melody. "We'll report back once we see what is going on."

"Hold on," Melody said. She pulled the small phone away from her ear and typed in the address as she read it from her computer. She hit "Send" and put the phone back to her ear. "You should have it now," she told Alex.

"We'll be out of here in about ten minutes," Alex said to Melody.

"I will buy you as much time as I can. We can check out the address on file first. Abby will be interested. Alex, I will not lie to her. I will not lose her trust. I will tell her I told you and you are going, but just to look, right?" she said.

Alex paused. "I understand, Melody, but we have to keep her safe. Tarkington will have our heads if we mess up."

Melody smiled as she said to Alex, "I know, and I know how he is, but I'm not sure if I want to piss off her or Michael either."

Alex laughed. "I said something similar once and I was right to do so," he said to Melody.

Melody told Alex, "I'll talk to Abby when she comes out. Will check in at 0800 hours."

"Got it. Melody, be careful," Alex said.

"Got it," Melody said back to Alex, and then they both hung up.

"Got what?" Abby asked Melody while drying her hair. "Who was that?"

"It was Alex," Melody said, and Abby came forward. "What?"

"We are going to split up," Melody told Abby. "We have two leads now. You and I will take one, they will take the other and just do recon. We'll then decide which one to hit. No one will go in without you."

Abby looked at her. "Would you lie to me?" she asked Melody.

Melody looked straight into Abby's deep blue eyes. "Never, and I think you know that. I swear on my love for Alan."

Abby looked out the window and at the beautiful lake under the rising sun. "Michael would have loved this view," she told Melody.

"I bet," Melody responded to Abby. "Alan says Michael is obsessed with sunrises. Something about them being the center of the universe."

Abby laughed and said to Melody, "Yeah, that is a

simplification. Michael believes if you watch the sunrise and sunset each day, you can start to appreciate the beauty of the world."

Abby was dressed in black cargo pants and a black tank top, along with a black long sleeve button down as a cover over it. She put on her boots and rung out her wet hair. Then she ran a comb through it and looked at Melody. "Are you ready to check out our lead?"

Melody looked at Abby and asked, "Should we get packed up?"

Abby smiled. "I'm already packed," and she picked up her small bag and laid it on the bed. "Travel light, ready for a fight," she said to Melody.

Melody cocked her head and asked Abby, "What?"

"Michael used to laugh and say that, Melody. When he went away, he would take a small bag and buy everything he needed, then he'd discard it all as he went. He said it kept him from having to spend any time thinking about what to take with him," Abby said.

"What about money?" Melody asked Abby.

"Michael was careful, and always had what he needed," Abby replied, as she waited for Melody to throw things in her bag.

Melody finished packing and walked to the door. "Done," she said to Abby.

Abby laughed and said to Melody, "Slowpoke, about time."

Abby and Melody walked out of the suite and took the elevator to the ground floor. As they did so, the bellman asked if they enjoyed their stay. "There's an amazing view," Abby said as they left the building.

Chapter 31

Alex had not been looking forward to this call.

"What the fuck do you mean, Abby is there too?" Tarkington screamed into the phone. "Are you the master of dumb-fuckery? Is there something seriously wrong with your head, boy?" he yelled at Alex.

"General," Alex started.

"That's right, you little twerp!" The General said to Alex. "You know how I got this fucking position? By making good decisions and not getting my superior's daughter killed!" Tarkington bellowed.

Rachel and Jim stepped back since they could hear Tarkington from several feet away. He continued to wail at Alex who had the phone away from his ear. They finally heard, "Are you there, dumbass?"

Alex stopped then answered the General. "Yep."

"What the fuck do you have to say for yourself?" Tarkington spat at Alex.

Alex was wound up. "First, she is your daughter, and she was ahead of this the whole way. She has a significant body count behind her already, and I was not going to be the one to get shot for trying to stop her," he told Tarkington.

"But she..." Tarkington started to say to Alex.

"I'm not done," Alex jumped in. "You know, General, that Abby can be strong-willed. I don't know where she got it, but she is also stubborn and pigheaded. She can't be reasoned with when she has a purpose. She was on a plane, and at least we got Melody in with her, but she came here, met up with a gunsmith, and is now in Muskegon, Michigan. She is looking to tangle with the guy who probably took her boyfriend. Some idiot named Jack Jennings. We are going to head to his overly guarded farm in the middle of nowhere and try to figure this thing out. I have already sent her in another direction, but she will do what she wants. If I threw her in irons and locked her up, I think she would eat right through the wall to get Michael back. You gonna come out here and stop her?"

Jim and Rachel quietly clapped their hands at Alex while Terry, Barbara and Ronnie nodded in approval.

"She killed people?" Sam Tarkington asked Alex.

"At least 7 confirmed right now," Alex told the General.

"Damn, I knew Abby was a chip off the old block," Tarkington said with a bit of glee in his voice. "Yes, I will be on my way. The guy, Jack, I have heard of him. He used to be with special forces. He got thrown out for liking it too much. He will be a good challenge. Get your asses over there and be careful," he told Alex then hung up.

Alex looked at his phone for a second. "That was weird."

Jim laughed. "What else is new?" he asked Alex.

"Well, let's get out of here and go figure this out," Alex told Jim.

Jim was exuberant, telling Alex, "We are off to find our Jack."

Alex laughed at Jim. "Very funny."

Jim looked at Alex then down to his pants and Rachel started giggling.

Alex looked at Jim. "What?"

"Would you look at the size of those "cahoonas?" Jim said to Alex while grinning from ear to ear.

Rachel broke out laughing. "I love the part when you said, 'I don't know where she got it'. I bet he was fuming," she told Alex.

Alex looked a little dumfounded and replied to Rachel. "No, he got pretty quiet after that."

"Really?" Jim asked Alex.

"Yeah, it was almost like he was proud of Abby for fighting her way out," Alex told Jim.

"Damn, I would be," Rachel said. "Abby has given me a girl crush and all," she told the guys. Jim looked at Rachel who told him, "Don't get all excited. It is just a saying."

Ronnie spoke up. "What do you mean though, Rachel?"

Rachel looked at Ronnie. "Have Barbara explain it to you when you hit puberty."

Ronnie looked at Barbara and she whispered in his ear. Ronnie giggled but turned red anyway.

Terry was ever the professional, and Jay was bringing up the rear. He was walking and scanning the area like they were going into battle.

Jim looked back and said, "Jay, I don't think anybody knows who we are here."

Jay looked at Jim seriously. "That's when it always gets bad."

Chapter 32

Larry sat in his room in the hospital. It was quiet. He was going to be fine. Flowers were next to him which he looked at while the IV slowly dripped into his arm. His wounds had been mostly superficial, except for his broken leg and a piece of shrapnel in it. He was lucky, really lucky. While lost in his own thoughts, the phone in the room rang and he picked it up.

"Larry," the voice said. "Is it Jack?"

Larry squeezed his eyes shut for a moment. He paused, then replied to the voice, "Yes."

"Did Abby see you?" the voice asked.

Larry paused again, then replied to the voice, "Yes."

The line went dead, and with a shaky hand, Larry hung up the phone.

Chapter 33

The GPS had them doing turns everywhere. The roads were strange, as they zigzagged through the city and went down a split road. A pristine veterans park was in the center, small flags adorning the area. It looked revered more than those of many cities dozens of times bigger. The park had bridges that were painted and pure. There were statues, of long-lost men, that could not be impugned because of their powerful messages. It was a testament to how people should see veterans. As they passed the park, Abby and Melody were silent, each considering their own internal demons.

"Who would have thought a state full of lakes would have a River Road?" Melody said to Abby as they turned on the road and headed due west.

"How far away is the second location after we check this out?" Abby asked Melody.

"Inside of forty-five minutes," Melody told Abby. "They are fairly close."

"Good," Abby said. "I know you think you are doing the right thing, Melody, but we know this is a wild goose chase."

Melody looked at Abby. "Do you think I would ever lie to you?"

Abby looked back at Melody. "No, but I think you picked the safer target for us."

Melody smiled. "Maybe, but maybe not. I have learned not to guess where things like this are concerned," she said to Abby.

"Smartest thing I have heard you say," Abby said. "Have you

heard from Alan?" she asked Melody.

"No," Melody answered Abby. "He was tracking down a potential plane wreck. He will be fine. I am sure the dogs are with him."

Abby laughed. "I wish we had them here," she said to Melody.

Melody smiled and told Abby, "We don't have to talk all the time. We both know that our jobs and our privacy are important."

Abby looked at Melody. "Already? Usually, girls are pretty protective for a while before getting all 'he can do what he wants to do' on their men."

Melody smiled as the GPS had them turn right and head down a scenic drive. "Yeah, we got to trust pretty fast. It is easier when you both know who the other is completely," she told Abby.

Abby asked Melody, "Did you read his file?"

"The parts that weren't redacted," Melody responded to Abby. The two girls glanced at each other and started laughing.

The trees were incredibly thick in this area. The voice of the GPS spoke and noted that they had arrived. Abby turned left into a driveway and was met by a solid gate. She and Melody got out of the car and looked around. They tried to see what they could through the thick brush and tree line, but they could not see more than a few feet down the winding driveway. Everything was impeccable. Abby looked at the gate. The bar was across it and locked into place in the frame, and there was also a bar that had spun and was locked into concrete in the ground. It was a great design and similar to something she was quite familiar with.

Abby walked to the console next to her car at the driveway. There was a keypad and a fingerprint reader. She put her finger on the reader. Melody jumped backwards as gears spun and the lower bar swung upwards. As it arced, the two side boards folded in upon themselves, becoming part of an elaborate set of lines in the superstructure. "Get in," Abby told Melody as she got in the car. As the two rode through thick trees and brush, suddenly there was a clearing. The view was breathtaking.

The house stood majestically in a large clearing. As they drove up the driveway, they could see Lake Michigan on both sides behind it. Abby got out of the car and Melody followed as they walked to the side of the house and looked out on what could only be described as an ocean. They went on to the back yard then and looked down the steep dune. A solid fence was around the house with a gate that led to the beach. Abby looked both directions, and though she could see people and houses, it was sparse. This was a place that could make a person smile on their darkest day.

"Do you know this place?" Melody asked Abby.

"I have never been here," Abby said as they walked to the front of the house. She then went up to the all too familiar door and typed in a code. The door unlocked and she pushed it open, "but I am home," she told Melody.

Melody had been to Abby and Michael's house with Alan only once, but as she walked in, she gasped. It was nearly identical! Sheets covered much of the furniture, but as Abby peeled back some of it, she saw the same tables she had picked out.

Abby looked out onto the familiar balcony to a view that she knew Michael would love. There was a difference in this house though. In the center, a small spiral staircase went up, and Abby ascended the stairs. It opened to a small room, perhaps 10' x 10', that looked out both to the east and west. There on the north wall, a picture. She smiled, cried, and set her jaw. The picture was of Abby and Michael with a sunrise behind them. It had been taken in the Caymans. There was the same one in Michael's wallet all of the time.

Melody came up the stairs and simply said, "Whoa!" but Abby was going down. She went to the main room, then came upon the lower staircase where she descended again. Melody nearly ran to keep up. The weight room, the walls, a perfect copy. Abby slid the weights into position and the wall clicked and swung open. She walked into the room as it began lighting up and went to the back case. There she touched a drawer and opened it. Inside, she removed a weapon that could only be out of a science fiction movie. The Vanquish 308 was topped with a massive scope. Abby then hit a second drawer as she handed the weapon to Melody. There she pulled out the Barret 50BMG.

"Umm, a little big for you?" Melody asked Abby.

"It is only if we need it," Abby told Melody as she reached in and grabbed three magazines and handed them to her. She then grabbed three for the Barret. "Let's go," she said. "Right place, but wrong place to find Michael. Let's go get him."

Melody smiled and looked at the lightly oiled Barret. "Right behind you, Abby."

As they reached the front door, Abby looked back at the view and told Melody, "I like this." She then closed the door and watched the incredible bolt system seal. She opened the trunk of the car then and stowed the rifles. "Ready for some fun?" Abby said as they got in the car.

Melody looked at her. "Ready as I'll ever be," she told Abby."

Chapter 34

As Alex and the group arrived at the edge of the property, they got out of the vehicles and met between the two. In this way, the two Suburban's offered some cover in the event of an ambush. They readied their tactical gear, and in mere minutes, they all looked like part of a finely-honed battle team. Jay was slightly out of place because of his size, but he too looked ready to walk into hell.

"Jay," Alex said. "You know you don't have to do this?"

"Shut up," Jay replied. "Do we have to go through this again?" he asked Alex.

Alex smiled, but it was Jim who said, "Stay with us, Jay. I know you know, but we have come a long way since we first met."

Alex looked at the map and spoke to Terry and Barbara. "I want you two on that hill. Barbara, you are spotting for Terry. You will be our eyes and ears. Jim, you and Rachel are point. Ronnie, you will swing, and Jay and I will cover the rear. Everyone, check your comms." The radios on their ears were attached to larger units in their suits. They looked like Secret Service models but had a range that went a bit further. Each of them checked in and Alex said, "Verified. We will commence when we hear you are in place, Terry."

They waited, crouched in-between the Suburbans. Five minutes passed and there was a click. It was Barbara, in place, but targets were partially obscured by cover. "Terry, stay on station. Barbara, find a better vantage. We are proceeding," Alex said.

"On it," came the reply from Barbara. The five of them worked their way through pine trees and ferns that were as thick as any jungle. As they entered the ticket of Jack pines, it became dark as the trees fought above them for any amount of sunlight.

Alex looked around. "I don't like this." He said to Jim, "The trees are thinning and we're sitting ducks."

"Damn right we are! Go back?" Jim asked Alex.

"Damnit, no, we are this far, but we need to spread a little, just in case," Alex replied to Jim. He then whispered to the group, and the five spread out and continued forward about twenty feet from each other.

The ground was covered with pine needles. Occasionally the sun would shine in, and the ferns would be brilliant green for a moment. Before them, the trees seemed to be clearing out and the group quietly moved forward. "Go silent, voices ahead," Alex told the group as he looked back and to the side, each person nodding as they saw him. They continued, one step at a time.

The voices got a little louder. Alex faced his palm behind him. Everyone stopped and crouched. He waited, put his hand to his ear and crouched as well. They all listened. Alex rose and moved forward just a little and then stopped and crouched again. He swung his arm backwards, and as the group moved forward they created a 100-foot wedge with each 20 feet off of each other. Alex moved up and was near the edge of the clearing.

As Alex watched, he circled his hand above him, and the four others came to him in his location. They crouched together and watched. The campus was bigger than he thought it would be. Domes were covered with dirt to each edge, and Alex bet there was at least some underground facilities. They saw 10 men at a range begin firing. They were all firing single shots at targets about 20 feet out. The sound was loud, making it hard to hear anything. The five watched closely as each of the men stopped and added another magazine. The firing never stopped, a slow methodic pulse hitting the targets over and over, until Alex noticed that there were no targets.

Suddenly Alex knew what was going on. "Fall back,' he said into the microphone, and as they all turned around, the trees came alive. There were at least 40 weapons trained on them from 30 different locations. As Alex spun around at the clearing, he saw the shooting had stopped, and the men who were firing were now on their flank. They were completely trapped.

Alex heard a voice in his headset. "Nice of you to join us. I would really prefer you drop your weapons, so we don't slaughter you, yet. Stand please." The five stood and uneasily dropped their guns. There were tense moments until a short, barrel-chested man walked toward them. He was dressed all in black with a weapon on both sides. "Thanks for joining us," he said. "We were wondering if someone would show up."

Alex looked at him. "I guess."

Jack laughed and said to Alex, "Good guess. How many more?"

"What you see is what you get," Alex said to Jack.

"We will find them. We homed in on your transmission. You may as well tell me," Jack told Alex.

Somewhere in the hill behind them, Terry took out his earpiece, crushed it, and signaled Barbara to do the same. She worked her way back with the earpiece in hand. Terry took it and crushed it then, picked up the pieces and put them in his front pocket. "We need to get some distance," he said, so the two of them worked backwards to a thicket right before the access road and in line with the Suburbans.

Jack was still with Alex and the group, far out of range of Terry and Barbara. "Let's come on up here. You can be our special guests," Jack said wryly to the group.

Jay looked at Jack. "Looks like your special guest is the Stay Puff Marshmallow man. Damn, you ate too many s'mores."

Jack looked back and responded to Jay, "Must have shared the bag with you."

Jay laughed. "Yeah, but I can diet and be cute. After you lose weight, you will still be ugly," he told Jack.

Jim laughed and said, "Dog still won't play with him."

Jack turned around and looked at the group. "You won't make me mad or get me to make mistakes. The mistake is you coming here."

Alex looked at the group, then at Jack. "Why did you take Michael?"

"You'll see," Jack said to Alex. "We've missed having him here, but you will do just as nicely."

Jim smiled. "Cannibals," he said to Jack.

Jack looked at the group and smiled. "Close enough." He then told the mass of soldiers behind them, "Bring them to the pens."

Jim looked at Jay. "Doesn't sound good."

Ronnie answered, "No, it doesn't."

Chapter 35

"This is it," Melody told Abby. They pulled off the main road into a short driveway and were greeted by two Suburbans in front of them.

Abby started backing up the vehicle and Melody asked, "What are you doing?"

"Melody, we need to back out and move off somewhere else," Abby said.

"But that is most likely Alex and the team," Melody told Abby.

"Exactly," Abby said. "We don't need to be bunched up. The more of a footprint we have in one area, the easier we are to track and determine entry points," she said to Melody.

Melody was silent for a minute and then said to Abby, "You are probably right, if there's an army."

Abby drove about one hundred yards and pulled to the other side of the road into a large lot marked, "For Sale." She got out, removed a small chain, and then drove the car through the opening. She kept driving for a few dozen feet more behind the chain and hid the car behind a thicket of trees and bushes. "This will give us at least some cover," Abby said to Melody. "Pick your poison and let's get moving."

Abby took out the Vanquish from its case. The scope made it possible to hit targets from an immense distance, and the accuracy of the weapon was beyond compare. She pulled strap from the briefcase, closed the case and set them aside. Abby then put on a flak vest and attached the magazines to the vest. She looked to the side of the car and Melody was doing the same thing.

"You know, I liked this job because I could solve problems and figure out riddles. This group just seems to clean up trouble," Melody told Abby.

"The world is full of trouble," Abby said to Melody. "Someone has to clean it up."

Melody looked grim. "I know, I was just always more of a problem solver. I can fight, I actually enjoy it sometimes, but the odds are nowhere near in our favor," she responded to Abby.

"Michael always says the odds are in your favor if you believe they are in your favor. If they're not, change the game. Maybe it is time we change the game," Abby said with a smirk to Melody.

"Sounds like a unique point of view," Melody told Abby.

"It works," Abby said to Melody.

The two started walking in the brush, then watched the road carefully, crossed it, and came up to the Suburbans. Abby and Melody were quiet and methodical. They checked the cars but didn't touch them. Melody knelt at the base and noted the tracks and the path forward through the trees.

"I am not sure I like going through open pines," Abby told Melody. "We would be sitting ducks."

"If they knew we were coming," Melody said to Abby.

Abby cocked her head and looked at Melody. "Larry? I think they know we are coming. Maybe Alex is the bait now. Hopefully he has cleaned Jack's clock, and we can walk in, get Michael and leave."

It was Melody's turn to look at Abby. "You really don't think it will be that easy, do you?

"Hell no," Abby said to Melody. "But a girl can dream."

Melody smiled, "Trying to lighten the mood, Abby?"

Abby looked at Melody and said, "Life is never really a game, but you have to laugh and play it like one." She took a few steps forward and heard a sound behind her. She swung the rifle around and pointed it directly at Barbara as Melody started to do the same." Abby looked at the woman. "Not the best move."

Barbara stopped and breathed for a minute. "Terry is high ground behind us. We are pretty sure the rest are captured but not dead," she told Abby and Melody.

"What makes you so sure?" Melody asked Barbara.

"We heard them until the buds were crushed," Barbara told Melody. "The leader Jack was on site. He said something about Michael but didn't say he was there, then he talked about taking the group to the pens."

"Pens?" Abby asked Barbara.

"It is what we heard," Barbara said. "We set up on the dune behind us, hoping they came for the cars so then we could work our way in," she told Abby.

Abby thought for a minute, then picked up the burn phone she had taken from the plane and pulled up a map of the area. She hit the satellite view and looked at the clearing the best she could. She smiled. "I have a suspicion this is not what we thought," she said to Barbara and Melody.

"Share," Melody said to Abby.

Abby smiled again and told Melody, "If I am right, they weren't looking for Michael to punish him, they were looking for a trophy."

"What?" Melody asked Abby.

"Give Barbara your guns and your phone," Abby told Melody, "and let's take a walk."

"Pardon me?" Melody replied to Abby.

Abby asked Melody, "Do you trust me?"

"Not really," Melody answered Abby. "I know a lot about you, and it pretty much leads me to believe that I shouldn't trust you too much."

Abby laughed. "A good move, but it is time to trust me and follow my lead, Melody. We are going to walk right in and find out what's going on. Hopefully, we will get Michael and the others out."

"With what?" Melody pleaded, looking with fear at Abby.

"With pure moxie, and then maybe a little ass kicking to back it up," Abby answered Melody. "Sometimes people just need a good ass kicking to be reminded they aren't in charge."

Melody shook her head and walked to the end of the Suburban.

"Take care of the rifles, and don't scratch them." Abby told Barbara. "Call my dad, let him know we are here. If we don't get out, he can torch the whole place and at least know I went out in style. I think he would get a kick out of it."

213

Melody and Abby headed into the woods, surrounded by ferns and jack pines. They walked straight towards the compound and conflict.

Chapter 36

Alex and the group were led to a large building at the edge of the clearing. Alex looked and saw that the clearing was fenced on all sides that he could see. Dozens of cars, storage buildings, old boats and other structures were all over the area. As Alex surveyed, he noticed bullet holes in the wood of many of the buildings.

The large building was surrounded by its own fences, and that is when Alex saw that it was set like a kennel. Two men were at the edge of two of the pens looking out. They looked worn and wore dirty camo, their bodies covered in grime and their faces filthy with neglect. Both men stared outward, having locked their hands in the chain-link. The fences extended all around the pen so there was no way to climb out or under. It reminded Alex of a poorly cared for kennel he once saw as he looked closer.

They were pushed into the main doors as Jay began howling "arrwooooooo" like some lost wolf.

"Shut up!" said a man behind Jay.

Jay growled like a dog then and the man swung at him. For someone so large, Jay moved surprisingly fast and twisted out of the way. The man, carried forward by momentum, slipped and fell on the concrete floor.

Rachel laughed, then Jim did, and then Alex and finally Ronnie.

Jack walked into the room behind them. "Put them in the cells," he told the men.

"Wait!" Alex said to Jack.

"Wait?" Jack said to Alex in a quizzical tone.

"Well, of course. It is obvious that you have something fun in mind here, right?" Alex strode forward looking over Jack.

"Yes, something fun. So, why should I wait?" Jack asked Alex.

"Easy," Alex said. "I am betting you are trying to train these idiots to be a little better at fighting, right?" he asked Jack.

"Something like that," Jack answered Alex. "You're pretty quick for a prisoner."

"Welcome to your best day ever!" Alex stated in the voice of a talk show host. "I have a bargain for you, Jack. The five of us will take on any fifteen of your men, on your course, no weapons. We win, you let us go. You win, well, you will prove you have some damn good soldiers."

Jack laughed at Alex. "I could do that anyway, one at a time, or use you for target practice. Shoot off your fingers or something creative."

Alex smiled. "Yeah, you could, but you like this place, right?" he asked Jack.

Jack smiled back at Alex. "It has faced worse than you."

"Has it?" Alex grinned. "You know we work for Tarkington?" he asked Jack.

Jack stopped for a moment and considered, then he asked Alex, "That supposed to mean something?"

"You are good when people play by the rules. I bet you have gotten a lot of people to test your little team, picking on mercs and agents. Without proof, no one can come after you," Alex told Jack as Jim looked at him wondering where he was going.

"We lose, I will call and tell the General that it was a bad lead and throw him off," Alex said to Jack. "But right now, the clock is ticking, and this place will be leveled by people who don't play by the rules you have been skirting around."

Jack glared at Alex. "Why should I believe you?"

Alex again smiled. "I am a man of my word. You remember what that is like?" he asked Jack.

Jack struggled for a moment then said to Alex, "I like the idea, but let you go?"

Alex looked at Jack and said, "My word is we will walk away and give you forty-eight hours to get out. Better than you have now."

There were murmurs by some of the men within earshot. Jack glanced back but then focused on Alex. "Your word," he said and put out his hand.

Alex took Jack's hand and shook it.

"Your five against my fifteen," Jack said to Alex.

"Exactly," Alex said back to Jack. "No cheating."

Jack looked at Alex and scanned his group. "Cheat? What you must think of me."

Alex turned to Jim and whispered, "I bought us some time."

"And maybe a serious beating," Jim said to Alex with a laugh. "But hey, sounds like fun."

Jack led the group out into the field and Jim yelled aloud, "Two teams enter, one team leaves! Welcome to Thunderdome!"

Both sides laughed.

Chapter 37

The two women walked unchallenged through the woods. "Are you sure this is a good idea?" Melody asked Abby.

"I understand what this place is, I think," Abby said to Melody as she jumped over a fallen pine tree.

"It would be nice if you shared with me since we are walking in together, Abby," Melody retorted.

Abby slowed and looked up at Melody. "A long time ago I proved to myself and to Michael, I could handle myself against almost anyone. What if they are doing the same. Training against the trained. They are just being a little more final than I was back then."

"So, why Michael?" Melody asked Abby.

"I doubt they really knew who he was," Abby started, "and I am betting they had some source of documents. If you ever saw Michael's file, most of it is blacked out so they made assumptions," she told Melody.

"I have a copy of the file if you would like to see it," Melody said to Abby. "It leads people to believe certain things but no details. It pretty much reads like instructions you get for build it yourself furniture."

"I bet," Abby said. "I am sure only Michael knows everything he did. His life was a whirlwind for a while. More jobs than he could ever complete until he suddenly stopped," she told Melody. A clearing was coming up ahead.

"Abby, are you sure about this?" Melody asked.

Abby looked at Melody. "No, but I am sure enough to put my life on the line. To me, it's worth it. Not just for Michael, but for the group now in there. I got Jay into this, and I will get him out too." They came to the edge of the clearing. There was no one anywhere. They scanned the area and could see the crowd in the distance next to tall fences, milling around and screaming loudly.

"I guess we know where the action is," Abby said to Melody.

"How do you want to do this, Abby?" Melody asked.

Abby stood tall, well, as tall as she could at 5'4" and walked straight into the clearing. "Straight shot, right in," she answered Melody.

Melody walked fast for a moment, her stride long, and caught up to Abby quickly. "Well, this will be fun."

Chapter 38

Alex and the group huddled to the side. They had taken off the flak vests and shucked most of their equipment that had not already been confiscated. They now stood in basic outfits. "We need to do this right," he told the others. "We can't afford to lose anyone. They have the numbers, but we have the skill."

"Maybe," Jim responded to what Alex said. "If we assume that we may be in trouble. Maybe they have stayed around because everyone else got cocky."

Alex considered for a moment. "I see your point, but I am betting we are a little better prepared than the others that have been brought here."

"What's the play then?" Jim asked.

Alex looked at his team, they were ready, willing, and more than able. They had faced a lot since he had put them together and always found a way to come out on top. He considered a moment then spoke, "Rachel, you and Jim will take point. Once you take someone down, Ronnie and Jay will keep them down and I will swing where we need it. This will get rough really fast. If one of us goes down, we will be hurting. We can't afford to drop even one of us. If anyone gets hit hard, fall back between the rest of us. Same if you just need a breather, fall in between. Let's keep it smooth and keep them off balance."

Rachel looked at Alex and Jim. "Any rules?"

Jim looked at Rachel. "What do you mean?"

"Alex is always telling us to keep them alive," Rachel told Jim.

"Not this time," Alex broke in, "They won't be playing with us. It's time to cut loose. No quarter, no mercy."

Rachel considered for a second. "Are you sure?" she responded to Alex.

Alex looked at the woman who was one of the most confident people he had ever met, "I am sure, the faster they are out, the faster we end this. Broken or dead, it means the same."

Rachel looked at the man who commanded her, "Broken or dead." She said in a solemn voice, but her eyes almost twinkled with anticipation.

The wind blew slowly across the field, a brisk breeze that warmed the soul but chilled the heart. Rachel's hair flowed in the wind a little. Alex and the team turned to face the 15 men a few dozen feet from them. Jack walked forward and Alex walked out to meet him. They faced off. Jack was short but obviously solid. The 14 others on his group were rough, with few of them being under six foot. Jack was a hefty contrast to them.

Alex smiled.

"What's so funny?" Jack asked Alex.

"Reminded me of a movie. I am expecting you to introduce your team as "Laser" and "Blazer" and so forth," Alex kept smiling.

"I doubt we need introductions," Jack said to Alex, "and I don't get your joke."

"You wouldn't," Alex said dryly to Jack. "I expect you to keep your word."

Jack asked Alex, "You still think you will win? What do you

think we do here?"

"You play against retired soldiers and veterans," Alex said to Jack. "It might seem real, but you just play."

"I doubt the hundreds of bodies here agree with you." Jack looked at Alex. "If you manage to win, I will let you go."

"And Michael?" Alex asked.

"Michael never made it here," Jack told Alex. "I owed him one for years ago, even though I have never met him. He stole a kill from me when I was in the service. I would have had an even 100 but he took the kill I had planned. The next day, they shipped me home, said I was too brutal. Me, too brutal, what a joke! Yes, I enjoyed taking out targets. Who cares? I got the job done. When I got back here, I knew things needed to change. I," he paused for a moment, "We, our group, will make a difference."

"Think so?" Alex asked Jack. "Maybe you picked the wrong group to take on this time."

Jack laughed at Alex. "Dozens have said that. Tired old men like you and your group. They made deals too, but they were quick, just like you will be. They bargained for one on one though. You gave us three to one. Every one of them trained well but they fell like they should have, like retired soldiers."

"Every one of you we kill won't bring back those veterans, but I hope it will give them peace," Alex scowled at Jack.

Jack looked at Alex. "Perhaps your deaths will give them peace as well. A horn will go off, and we will fight. No rules, no nothing. One team will win, and one will lose."

"Sounds good to me," Alex said to Jack.

"This is to the death," Jack told Alex.

"I agree," Alex said to Jack, and then he walked back to his group.

As Alex reached Jay, Jim, Rachel and Ronnie, he was grim. "Kill them all."

"What did Jack say?" Jim asked Alex.

"If Jack was telling the truth, there are over one hundred veterans buried here," Alex responded to Jim.

"Check the anger at the door, Alex. He was trying to get under your skin. He knew that would make you mad, anger breeds mistakes." Jim retorted.

"When the horn sounds, it will be on," Alex stated. "Fall back and make them come to us," he told the group.

A giant air horn sounded and the fourteen men with Jack moved forward at a steady pace. They did not run, but they were not going slowly either. They apparently thought it was going to be quick and easy.

"Change of plans," Alex said to the others. "Let's put them on the defensive."

"Amen!" Rachel responded to Alex.

The first three men of Jack's group were moving toward Rachel and Jim as they moved up. Rachel was used to fighting three on one or more at the base, but she could truly cut loose now. As the first man reached for her, she grabbed him by the throat. She wasn't at all cautious and forced her fingers around his windpipe and then pulled forward. The man tripped in her direction, but her grip was faster and his esophagus came faster than that. He grabbed at his throat as he fell. Rachel did not stop moving as she slung blood from her hand. The second man was holding on to Rachel but she pulled loose, and after letting the first man fall, her palm went straight into the second man's nose. It was crushed and he fell back.

Jim was on the third man before he could react to what was happening next to him. He simply grabbed the man by the arm, and as he pulled forward, rolled in and leaned on his elbow. The joint snapped with a throaty crack and the man screamed in agony. Jim grabbed him as he fell and threw him over his shoulder, where Ronnie proceeded to hit him in the face like a hyperactive UFC fighter. He smashed the man's head with his fists over and over. Alex pulled Ronnie up and Ronnie kept pummeling for a moment on air. "He's out, get ready."

Twelve men were left. Alex glanced at Jack, who stepped back and yelled for his team to fall back. Rachel would not let that happen. She grabbed the closest man to her and pulled him towards her by the collar. As he turned to face her, he started to swing, but Rachel was much faster. She took hold of him by his beard and his ponytail and spun his head. The pop could be heard across the entire fenced area, and the man's head now faced to the rear of his body.

Jim was sparring with another man who was throwing punches and spin kicks as fast as the eye could see. He held with him, then as the man kicked forward, Jim turned sideways, grabbed his leg and twisted it. As he did so, the man fell to his stomach, following the leg-spin. Jim shifted on top of him then, grabbed the man's forehead and pulled backwards, cracking his neck again with an audible pop. The man went limp.

Ten men of Jack's group were left. Jim and Rachel fell back

to the rest of their group. Jim looked down at the man Ronnie had beaten mercilessly. "Good job, Ronnie," he said, and patted Ronnie on the back as they turned to face the remaining men. The two groups were about forty feet from each other where Jack had fallen out of range of Jim and Rachel.

Alex yelled, "Give up, Jack! Let us go! No one else need die!"

Jack was whispering to his group, then two men split to the left and two to the right. The remaining six began moving forward with Jack, all of them walking towards Alex and his group.

"Break right, double-time," Alex said in a low voice. The entire team headed to the right, going after two of the men of Jack's group who had swung around a small storage shed. Jim and Alex each took a side of the shed. As they did, the two men came around face to face with Jim, who just jumped sideways and kicked them both. The three fell to the ground, but Jim spun into a kip and was on his feet in an instant. He kicked the first man in the chest and felt ribs break as the second man grabbed his leg and yanked up hard. He caused Jim to lose his balance, and as he fell to the ground, the man grabbed for his head. He had not seen Jay come up behind him though. The vicious uppercut punch that Jay hit the man with lifted him completely off the ground. He fell back hard and did not move.

The group turned as they saw Jack's two men, who had gone in the direction to the left, jump Rachel who was behind the others. The first man was at least four hundred pounds and dove on her. The group heard a loud "oof," but as the second man began to kick her, he suddenly fell. Rachel had grabbed his ankle and pulled it from under him.

When Jim first met Rachel, she told him she worked out at least twice a day. Her muscle mass was impressive, and Jim knew how strong she was, since they had grappled dozens of times. As he watched, Rachel lifted the 400 lb. man off of her in a straight press. As she did so, the man flailed while Ronnie struck him over and over, then grabbed him and pulled. Between the two of them, the man rolled to the side and then Rachel stood up and dove on him. She went berserk as she hit his face over and over again. "Who the fuck do you think you are, you little shit?" She screamed at the man as she kneed him in the groin and continued to beat his face. Skin broke and the man's face began bleeding. Alex yelled, "He's out!"

Rachel looked at Alex. "He needs to stay that way!" she said, and she brought back her arm and hit him powerfully in the neck. The man was down, but suddenly blood began to gurgle and he began to convulse and choke on his crushed windpipe. Rachel stood and fell into the group as Jay pulled back with them.

Rachel was limping. Alex looked at her. "You ok?"

"Ribs, sir," she answered Alex. "I am betting at least two broken from the fat man," she puffed.

Jay looked at Rachel and checked her side. He lifted her shirt and said, "Ouch, maybe three. That will bruise bad."

"Hang behind us, Rachel. We will take point," Jay said, and he and Jim moved forward. Alex covered their backs and Ronnie moved from side to side.

Six men of Jack's group remained and for some reason had pulled back. Alex was curious as to why he had fallen back when they were on the defensive but considered that for all their practice, they were not tactic ready. Alex was feeling better. The odds were almost even. Alex yelled again, "We can end this now, just let us go!" With a yell the six men rushed in on them then, Jack in the lead, smashing into Alex.

"We will not lose!" Jack yelled as he hit Alex in the jaw with a massive punch. Alex was pinned and had no leverage. Jack hit him again, nearly taking his head off. Alex saw stars and was dizzy. He felt his eye swell. A third punch pounded Alex, but he partially rolled with this one and it appeared to bounce.

Jay grabbed at Jack's arm from one side, Jim from the other, and threw him back. Jack stood up and saw the last of his men out cold or dead on the ground. Alex slowly stood. Jack wiped his face. He looked at the four men and one woman and spat on the ground.

"This is what I wanted all along, an actual challenge," Jack told Alex.

"We win, or do we have to kill you too?" Alex asked Jack, blood running from his face.

Jack laughed. "Oh, great job," he said, then raised his hand and twenty men ran to the field with weapons pointed at Alex and his group.

"I should have expected," Alex said. "Idiots like you never keep their word," he told Jack.

"Oh, Alex, don't be so naïve," Jack said. "I can't let you go."

"Again, no honor. How can these people trust you?" Alex asked Jack in a mock tone.

"Easy," Jack said. "We discussed it before this fight started. If I had died, they were to kill you and move on. As it is, we will pack you up and head out," he told Alex.

Jim looked at the group and said to Jack, "Maybe we will just fight anyway and see how many we can take before we die."

"That would be stupid as well," Jack told Jim. "You might have a chance to escape, and you won't be able to do that dead."

There was silence for a minute, silence and obvious frustration. It was Ronnie that broke the silence. "I know the General will find you and kill you. If, by some miracle he does not, Michael will," he told Jack.

"Taking us on isn't the same as stealing a kill. Michael won't do a damn thing and is probably dead anyway. And Tarkington? Well, we will be long gone within the hour, and it will take him months to find us here," Jack said. He looked at Ronnie who frowned in the corner. "Don't pout. We will have fun together."

"You are a liar," Ronnie said quietly to Jack as his fists balled up.

"Aww," Jack said. "I will do whatever I need to do to keep my group safe. If that means lying to you to better the group, it's a small price to pay," he told Ronnie.

Ronnie launched forward with raw anger and swung towards Jack. A dozen rifles turned and were trained on him as Jim grabbed the younger man around the chest and pulled him back. "He's not worth it, Ronnie. We'll get our chance."

"You might get a lot of chances," Jack told Jim. "We have been working towards independence for quite some time. We just didn't have anyone good to train with properly. The veterans, mercs and ex-assassins were one thing, but they all were nothing compared to the training we already had. Sure, there was an occasional slip and someone good came in, but I never had an issue finding someone we trained more effectively to show them the way to the woodpile."

"I still don't understand why," Alex said cautiously to Jack

229

while looking to the back of the crowd.

"It's easy," Jack said. "Have you looked at the world?" he asked Alex. "Women don't know their place, men won't put them there. Television and the internet have created a world full of pansies. Our movement will grow, and now we will send out more and more tendrils to create dissension. We'll eventually take back this country. We will start here in Michigan, then work our way to surrounding states. Not through force, but through easy acts. We will fight as we need to, and we will win, and as we do, we will win over the groups that hate all the immigration and integration."

"Sounds like Adolf is in the house," Jim said to Jack.

"Not quite so bad," Jack stated dryly back at Jim. "People just need to know their place, and those that don't, well, we can take care of that."

"Another case of petty revenge and another wannabe dictator," Alex said.

Rachel looked at Jack. "You will not be putting me in the kitchen."

"Wouldn't think of it," Jack said. "You will fight until you lose and be a shining light for all the women who think they can win. We will record your last fight and your death will truly show that men are superior."

"Fuck you!" Rachel said to Jack. "I will kill every one of you."

"Oh, Rachel. I can rotate people in and out until you fall asleep, and then finally, you will die," Jack said.

A loud voice came from behind. There was a group of women with Abby in the front of them all. "So, you want women to be slaves? All of these women too?" she yelled at Jack.

Jack was stunned for a second and then there was recognition. "Ms. Tarkington I presume. I have seen your pictures at Larry's. Nice of you to join us."

"Answer the question!" Abby yelled at Jack.

"No, not slaves, partners, and as partners they have their part. The men will lead, the women will follow, as it is meant to be," Jack told Abby.

Abby looked around at the women. Most of them bowed their heads in submission. A few watched closely. Jack yelled, "Bring her to me!" Several men walked through the group and pushed the other women down. They grabbed Abby and walked her to the front of the group where Jack, Alex and the teams had stood.

"Alex, nice to see you. You seem to have made a mess out of things," Abby said, indicating the bodies all over the area. "Nice handiwork."

"We wanted to make an impression," Jim said and laughed.

"But this guy lied, and he is going to keep us here. He had said that he was going to let us go. He's a bold-faced liar!" Ronnie screamed.

"Will you stop calling me a liar?" Jack yelled at Ronnie. "This is war. Things have to be done."

Abby looked straight at Jack and stared at him. "I will end up watching you die, or worse, watching my father take you away."

Jack started laughing and slapped Abby across the face. She fell to the ground hard but got to her knees right away. That is when she noticed the red dot on the grass.

Chapter 39

Alex and the team moved to help and there was a ruckus as large weapons were brought to bear on the six of them. "Leave her alone," Alex yelled, "Coward!"

Abby held her hand up at Alex and stood, turned and looked at Jack. Her lip was red from the backhand, but not bleeding. "That all you got?"

Jack looked at her and his group. The members of the group looked at each other as well. There were murmurs in the crowd.

Abby looked at Jack and saw the blink of a red laser in his beltline. The light pulsed, 1, 4, 3. Abby started laughing. She laughed hard. "I don't need to talk to you, Jack. How about we do this? How about I kick your ass in front of all your little peeps here and show them the shit you are shoveling. A girl, kicking your ass. No more games, no more lies. You and me. The others can watch, but when I knock you on your ass, you will let us all go," Abby said as she turned to Jack, his followers and Alex's group.

"Let me kick his ass!" Rachel yelled. "I will slaughter the little man."

Abby looked at Rachel, her eyes gleaming. "This is my fight. After all, I am just a little tiny girl. What do you say, Jack? You man enough to take me and not an old man, or have to cheat 3 to 1? Just you and me."

"We don't have time for this," Jack told Abby. "Bring her. We will finish this later," he said to his men.

"How about we finish it now?" Abby said to Jack. "No need to make these people wait to see what a big man you are. I am sure you can make short work of me." Abby was stalling, buying time for

Melody to complete her task. She was happy and excited inside though. Michael was alive and he was here! No one else would have given her a 143 from a distance. He was watching out for her, as always, but letting her lead. Well, for the moment anyway.

Abby knew the situation was precarious, and it would not take much for them all to end up dead or at least some of them. But now, now she had the advantage. "C'mon Jack, you know you are a tough guy. Let's dance," Abby said. She looked around and saw that there were about 50 men spread all over the quad. Right now, there was no advantage to be had, but she knew with Melody and Michael in her pocket, she would be able to pull this off.

Jack looked at his group. The murmurs were breathing with a life of their own. "Sure," Jack said looking around at the group. "Why not? This will only take a few minutes."

Abby walked up towards Jack. He put out his hand to shake hers, but she slapped it away. Jack tried to grab her, but she stepped back out of his reach. "Sorry, Jack. Not falling for that one."

Jack furled his brow, obviously irritated, as he moved in on Abby. He was focused, and his black short hair glistened with sweat from the earlier fight. He jumped at Abby, and she sidestepped. She swung into him at his leg and tried to break his knee, but the blow glanced, and she slid off of him. Jack staggered and fell to one knee. Catlike Abby moved away quickly, and Jack cursed as he got up and moved back towards her.

Abby knew she had to be patient, work the opponent. Michael had taught her to watch for the opening. He said that fighting with a superior opponent was like dancing, you just had to be patient and watch. When the opportunities come, take them, and never before then. Abby held the thought as Jack ran at her. She sidestepped. He tried to grab her, but she slipped away. He was expecting her to counter and was trying to get her in between that counter.

Jack was faster than Abby would have guessed. He came forward again for her, and this time as he feigned, he let his guard down on his right. Abby let him go by and spun with a round kick into his ribs from the back. Jack fell face first on the ground.

Abby smiled and looked at Alex, who nodded. Jim pointed back to Jack, and Abby turned to see him getting up quickly and running for her. As he dived for Abby, she grabbed his head and flipped over him. As she came down, he again landed face first, and Abby put all her weight into the fall, driving her boot into Jack's calf.

Jack spun over and tried to trip Abby, but she was already moving and had gotten out of the way. A few of Jack's men applauded. Jack glared at them all. "Clapping?" he yelled. "For her?" He seethed with more obvious anger. Looking back at his quarry Jack slowed and moved in. Abby tried to stay out of his reach. Jack dove and got a hold of her arm, or so he thought. Abby was quick and lithe, and she twisted out, even though the strain was tremendous. Jack was holding air. Using the moment to her advantage Abby spun and kicked him in the face, once, twice, three times. Jack bellowed in anger and started swinging blindly at Abby.

Abby backed off. Her arm tingled, but she could use it. She favored it, and though it was her right arm, it would not matter. She was counting in her head.

Jack was running at Abby again, and when he reached her, he got fully kicked in the face another time. He fell back, she kicked again, spinning in a revolving round kick that pummeled Jack in the face three then four more times.

Jack staggered, then backhanded Abby, mostly missing, but connecting enough to make an impact. She fell backwards and Jack advanced. Jim started pushing forward, but guns trained on him quickly.

As Jack reached Abby, she knew he had a huge advantage, and she readied herself to fight again. She was the little ship that was going to win not because it was 100% but because it was 200% all the time.

At that point, the kennel exploded. A huge plume of flame rocketed into the air, then each of the houses to the side began to explode. One after another, the buildings that housed everything were reduced to splinters. Everyone looked on as the black smoke flew into the sky. Jack kicked Abby in the side, then he walked to one of his men and wrenched the AR-15 from his hands. He looked at Abby, unbridled fury in his eyes. He pulled back the slide on the weapon and aimed it right at her.

Abby considered for a moment. It had been a good fight. The plan had worked perfectly. Seeing all of the men gathered watching Alex and his team fight, Abby had decided to move forward while Melody found a way to blow up what was there. In the process, she would release the prisoners they saw in the pens, and Abby would get the women up to the fight as well.

The plan was going perfectly, except Jack was swinging a gun to bear on Abby. She knew she might be in the last seconds of her life. Abby thought about her father and their difficult life together, about all the special moments she had had in her life. Mostly she thought about Michael, her friend that had become her love, her love that had become her life. It was interesting how slow the world seemed to be moving, and how slowly Jack moved the gun. Everything seemed as though it was in slow motion. The barrel could not be moving more than a millimeter at a time. As she looked at the weapon training on her she saw the gun light up, gleaming with a bright red light for only a moment, then it exploded in that same slow motion, wood splintering and the weapon slamming into Jack.

Abby looked at Jack, holding the broken weapon with his bloody hands, and jumped forward. Her ribs hurt but she didn't care. As she jumped, she grabbed Jack's head and forced it down, directly into her knee. Jack fell and rolled on the ground. He tried to get up, he struggled against the inevitable, but fell back, unconscious.

Abby stepped in front of everyone. "Listen to me! Drop your weapons and no one else needs to die!"

Abby heard the words, "Fuck you!" from the side. A man started to raise his weapon, only to fall to the ground, dead. The man next to him spun to face the woods, lifted his weapon, and he too fell to the ground dead. Two other men spun and started to point their weapons to the woods, only to fall quickly with a single shot between their eyes.

Murmurs began to rise in the crowd but no one else was moving.

Abby yelled again. "Everyone drop your weapons and put your hands on your head! No one else needs to die here today!" Men, who a short time ago were braced to take over the country, looked at her and the pile of bodies made by the small group. They looked at Jack lying on the ground, and then over to the men who had just tried to fight, now on the ground as well. Slowly each and every man began to drop their weapons. Both men and women placed their hands on their heads.

Abby looked back at Alex, his face now puffy and blue with the beating he took from Jack. "I always wanted to say that. Think you can help me clean up?" she asked Alex.

Alex tried to smile, but his face was not cooperating. Jim stepped up, and Terry and Ronnie headed out to the group and began policing the weapons. Rachel stepped up to Abby. "Not bad," Rachel said as she looked at Abby up and down, "not bad at all for a midget." Abby laughed and Rachel giggled as she moved out to the group to clean up as well.

Abby turned and saw Melody walking with two ragged men from the pens. Melody walked up to her while Alex walked over to the men. "Good job, Melody!" Abby said. "How did you get that big of an explosion?"

"They provided me an ample supply of C-4 in the pen," Melody replied to Abby. "It was in some boxes to the side. Didn't take me long to set things while you moved the women up to the fight," she explained. "I saw part of your fight, and when I saw things take a turn, well, I decided it was time to blow things up."

"Thanks, Melody," Abby said.

"I just don't get one thing." Melody questioned Abby. "His weapon exploded. How did you do that?"

Abby looked down, smiled, and looked up with a tear in her eye and told Melody, "Michael is here. He is alive."

At the edge of the clearing, Melody and Abby turned to see Michael, Terry, and Barbara walking towards them. Terry was holding Michael's Barret while Michael walked with the Vanquish strung across his chest.

Abby could contain herself no longer as she ran to Michael, holding her side. As she reached him, she hit him in the chest.

"What was that for?" Michael asked Abby with surprise in his voice.

"I had this, and why didn't you call me?" Abby said as she looked up at Michael with a gleam in her eyes.

"I know you had this," Michael said, "but Terry was getting all antsy. He must have had to pee," he told Abby. "As far as calling you, umm, I don't have your number."

"I am gonna' kick your butt!" Abby said to Michael with a grin on her face.

Michael turned a little. "This butt?" He danced around, and as Abby started to chase him, he grabbed her and held her. "I missed you."

"I love you," Abby told Michael. "I thought I had lost you."

Michael looked into her eyes, his blue eyes shimmering in the sun. "I know. That's what I get for going to the shower unarmed. Oh, and I love you more," he said to Abby.

Abby laughed, then she and Michael walked back to the encampment as Alex and his team continued to collect weapons and secure the captives.

Chapter 40

Tarkington arrived in a frustrated mood. He was irritated at the Muskegon airport for trying to make them wait to land their plane. They did get to land right away though, after he told the air traffic controller they were going to do so, even if it meant landing on top of their precious little prop planes.

Although the plane had been met with airport security, the National Guard in the area was driving out to the plane at the same time. A short colorful discussion later, the airport security was backpedaling and apologizing to the Guard for the delays.

Then there were the cars. Tarkington had Sarah call ahead and get four Suburbans from a local rental company. What waited for them were four minivans instead. They were very nice, but they were red, yellow, green and black, which made the General say, "They make us fucking look like a bad day at a stop light." There were no other vehicles though, so they loaded up and headed out, only to find that the map was less than accurate in many places. At one point, the map had them turn in a circle. One of Tarkington's guards pulled up Google Maps then and got directions, which solved that problem.

As the minivans pulled in, the drives were already filled with cars, so a local police officer flagged Tarkington to turn around. This last affront was enough to push the already cranky General off the range. He opened the side door of the black minivan and stepped out of it. He then walked up to the officer and proceeded to berate not only him, but his mother, his father, his dog, his next-door neighbor, and a few relatives the man may not have known he had. In the end, his guards explained the situation far more eloquently, and the four minivans were directed through as the officer stood wondering why he had been put out front in this circus.

As they reached the clearing where the acronyms ran rampant, Tarkington saw FBI, DEA, ATF, and a bunch of plain vans that belonged to assorted other agencies. They were all trying to get a part of this massive debacle. In the center of it all stood Alex with his team, directing each of the groups to different areas. To the side stood a group of men and women being protected by the soldiers of the National Guard. Sitting in a chair in the middle of it all were Michael, Jay, and Abby, talking to each other like it was Sunday tea and no one else was on the field.

Tarkington walked up to Alex. "What the fuck ran over you?" he said tersely, looking at Alex's face and the butterfly bandages holding portions of it together. "You look like a Smurf who ate too many grapes."

Jim laughed hard and said to the General, "I was just saying the same thing."

"I don't remember pulling your string," Tarkington spat at Jim.

Jim laughed harder and told Tarkington, "I don't remember inviting you to our party." Alex put up his hand and Jim, still laughing, turned and walked to the group taking care of firearms with the ATF.

"Took a few hits, sir, but none worse for the wear," Alex told the General. "We have a lot of work here. It looks like they have been stockpiling for quite some time."

"Anyone hurt bad?" Tarkington asked Alex.

Alex pointed to a row of body bags. "None on our side. We did have some casualties from Jacks's group, sir," he responded to Tarkington.

"To be expected," Tarkington told Alex. "I understand that Michael was in the middle of all of this and ended it as well."

"Actually, sir, in my opinion, Abby ended it all. Michael just backed her up in a way that was more forceful than she could be on her own," Alex said to Tarkington in a matter-of-fact tone. "You should also know that she and Melody not only saved our asses, but they saved a considerable number of noncombatants too."

"Hmm," Tarkington huffed. "How do we break out of this and let the other groups handle it?" he asked Alex.

"Simple," Alex replied to the General. "We just walk away."

Tarkington looked at the group operating efficiently as people were processed and other agencies directed. He looked over at the small group he had assembled and realized they were in charge but would walk away at his order. "Carry on, Brown," the General said as he walked towards Michael, Jay, and Abby. As he did so, Michael glanced his way and Jay stood. Abby stood as well and walked over to him.

"How are you holding up? I hear from Sarah you are fighting through it, and I see you walking here today," Abby said to her father.

"I will push through whatever hell comes my way," Tarkington told Abby.

Abby laughed. "Typical answer. You could barely walk a few months ago. You are sweating it now. What are you doing here?" she asked him.

"My job, Abby, my job," Tarkington said. "It takes a lot to keep this country safe. I can't take a vacation."

"Well, don't worry, I did your job this time," Abby said to her father. "I kept the world safe from a nut because he went too far."

"I am proud of you, Abby," Tarkington said.

"Don't be. I didn't do it for you, or for the country. I did it for Michael. I did it for the person who protected me all the time, and it was my turn to do it for him. Be happy, take care of this whacko, but don't think for a minute I was doing this for you," Abby told Tarkington. She then turned to Michael and said, "Can we get out of here?"

Jay and Michael both stood. "Nothing keeping us here," Michael replied to Abby.

"Abby," the General started, "I do understand. I just..."

"Save it, Dad. We are fine. The world is fine. You have plenty to do here. Make sure you throw Jack somewhere that is deep and impossible to get out of, okay?" Abby turned to Michael. "I have the Aston Martin. What did you drive?" she asked.

"A rental. I got full coverage on it so we could blow it up," Michael told Abby.

"Michael, we need to take it back," Abby said.

"Jay, will you drive the other car?" Michael asked.

Abby, Michael, and Jay walked out towards the woods where the small access road waited. As they did so, Melody ran to Abby. "Where are you going?" she asked.

"Meet us there when you can," Abby told Melody. "You know where. Bring the team but not my Dad."

"Abby," Melody said. "Thank you for everything." She

looked at Michael. "Thank you, too. I feel like I know you from being around Abby, or at least I know you a little more. Thank you. Is Alan with you?"

"He is safe," Michael told Melody. "He ripped his stitches, so I dropped him off. I didn't need his guts falling out in the middle of a fight. I am sure he has stitched himself back up and is playing with the dogs now."

Melody smiled at Michael. "Thank you."

Abby looked at Melody. "Don't worry. We will see you soon."

Michael eyed Alex, blue and beaten from the fight earlier, and nodded. Alex tried to smile again, but it came across as a grimace. Still, he nodded back.

Melody walked back towards the group of men milling around who were now pulling Jack up. "You asshole!" Jack screamed. "This was the way the world needed to be, and you and your bitch messed it up!" he shouted at Michael.

Michael looked at Jack, laughed, then walked away with Abby and Jay, disappearing into the woods.

As they left, Alex looked down at Jack. "You really don't know him, do you?" he said.

"I know his type," Jack said. "All big and bad on the outside, but all talk and no action," he said about Michael.

Alex looked behind Jack. The area was clear. He looked at the woods, tugged his ear a little, heard a whiz, and looked down to see Jack screaming about his ear. "I guess he heard you," Alex said. "Next time whisper."

Epilogue

The waves beat upon the beach as heartily as any ocean. Lake Michigan is a large lake, and ocean of fresh water. Many people have never been to see it, to feel it, to experience it on a calm day, or see it's fury when it's stormy. Today it was sunny and warm, and Abby and Michael sat on the balcony watching the waves roll in and feeling the breeze slide across them.

"You should have told me about this place," Abby said to Michael. "I would have asked to spend more time here."

"It was just finished a few months ago," Michael replied. "We really had not slowed down enough to go anywhere," he told Abby.

"We found time now, Michael," Abby said.

Michael laughed and said to Abby, "Not exactly how I wanted to get here."

There was a knock at the door, and Michael went and opened it halfway, most of his body behind the door. It was Alex, Melody, Jim, Rachel, Ronnie, Terry and Barbara.

"There goes the neighborhood," Michael said. "First time I met you, Alex, I blew up my house. I won't have to again, will I?"

"No. Umm, can we come in?" Alex asked Michael.

Michael laughed. "Habit," he told Alex and opened the door. As they all walked in, Jim noticed the FN57 in his hand, which he moved behind his back quickly. "Habit as well," Michael said.

"We picked up the two guys out in the middle of nowhere," Alex said. "Your pilot took a team back out there and they are singing like little birds. The two of them are worried you will come back after them, Michael."

"Good job," Michael said to Alex as he placed the FN57 back inside a small wooden shelf and folded it up.

"We also found the contractor who set it all up," Alex continued. "Your description made us go down a few paths, but those two guys gave us a name, and he spilled pretty quickly. Apparently, they didn't have much to go on. Jack just tied an address to your old file and somehow found you. I am betting it is a fluke, so don't blow the house up." Alex said the last part sarcastically to Michael, but he meant it all.

Abby walked into the house in a small red bikini and thin cover. She was greeted by the group immediately.

Alex took Michael to the side and Jim joined. "We are pretty sure we got most of them, but they had said the network is pretty big. So, I would stay sharp for a while, just in case."

"I will not be taken so unaware again," Michael told Alex. "New cameras, smarter, that track people and give me warning faster."

"What's next?" Jim asked Michael. "Are you staying or going?"

"I would have said we were going back to Dubois, but I sent Jay home to Janet. Abby and I will stay here a few weeks, then head back. This whole experience was good for us. She held together. I trust her more than life itself so I let her do what she needed to do until I needed to be there. She has always been worried about that with me, so it's even better between us now," Michael said.

Abby yelled at Michael, Jim and Alex. "Let's go outside and watch this!"

"What?" Michael asked Abby.

"I told Melody to go walk on the beach, Michael," Abby said.

Michael laughed and they all walked out onto the balcony. Barbara tickled Ronnie playfully as they watched Melody round the end of the small path. Two giant wet mops of fur ran past her, then around her, and then she tripped on their legs. Alan walked up to the now prone Melody laying on the ground and extended his arm. Melody looked up at him in his Khaki shorts and tank top. She could see the tightly bandaged arm and leg and rippling muscles as he pulled her off the ground effortlessly with his good arm. Melody reached up to Alan and they kissed. The dogs ran around them then dashed into the waves, swimming and playing.

Abby, Michael and the team watched from the balcony until Rachel finally said, "Well, that was sickening and mushy. Do you have any grub here?"

Michael flipped on the grill and grabbed Jim and Alex. "Help me out," he said as they walked into the house.

"The guns, where did they end up?" Michael asked Alex as the three of them went into the kitchen.

"Four of them were found. Larry says there is a fifth. Melody had him put in protective custody. He is pitching a fit about it but cooperating," Alex told Michael.

"Where will Jack end up?" Michael asked Alex as he took out a giant stack of steaks from the refrigerator.

"Umm, do they stock this all the time?" Jim asked Michael.

"No. I called and had food delivered last night," Michael told Jim. "Jack?"

"The General considered having him killed," Alex said, "but he will end up in Gitmo," he told Michael.

"Having him killed would have been better," Michael said. "Did he ever really know me?" he asked Alex.

"Apparently not. Oh, and nice job, Michael. You removed his earlobe perfectly," Alex said with a laugh.

"I barely remember him," Michael told Alex. "Tarkington had sent me in to mop up a mess in the middle of nowhere. Apparently, the targets were double designated on purpose to keep from missing anyone. The idea was if one of us missed, the other would clean it up. I was just a little faster than Jack, finished my list and started working his."

"After reviewing things with Jack, he was unaware of really who you were or even your relationship. That was until he got ahold of some files. We are working with the idea that Cassie released them and caused this whole thing. Tarkington is having more pictures taken and sent to her cell. I think he is more driven by that than anything right now," Alex told Michael.

Alex and Jim carried out the stack of steak and chicken and Michael began placing it on the grill. He stacked all the meat he had brought on one side and put it on low, then he put potatoes and vegetables on the other side at a higher temperature. He closed the grill and kept talking. "What do we need to do to stop being interrupted from our retirement?" Michael asked.

"I really wish I knew." Alex scratched his head. "I mean, you have a file a mile long, Michael, and it seems you may be the only one who can work through it. You are safe as long as people don't open the files."

"How can we get the files wiped?" Michael asked Alex.

"We tried pulling them all, but there were backups, and backups of the backups," Alex answered Michael. "It is a long tight system. The good news is most of your files are redacted, and we were able to plug the sale up here that Melody followed. So, you should be safe here for a while," Alex said.

Michael looked at Alex and asked, "Dubois?"

"Good guess is that some people may know, but it was a fluke. I would say it is safe too. Even your Ivel house is probably safe now. The real estate transactions were easier to shut down. They were older systems, not as many redundancies. Unfortunately, Tarkington's group has been under surveillance for a long time, so there are numerous watchdogs on it," Alex stated. "I wish I could say there was no trace of you, Michael, but it is hard in today's digital world."

Michael took out some tongs as the dogs bounded onto the landing below the balcony and shook off their fur. The water reached many of them and Rachel reacted with "oeeewww!"

Alan and Melody, arm in arm, walked up to the landing. They then proceeded up the stairs to the balcony area and opened the gate. The dogs were behind Alan. He turned and pointed. The dogs' responded to his gesture and sat then lay at the bottom of the stairs.

"I wish I could train Ronnie that well," Rachel said.

"Just takes practice," Alan told Rachel.

"Hey," said Ronnie, reacting to Rachel and Alan's words.

Abby was the gracious hostess and brought out a bucket of beer. They were craft beers from a variety of the local brewers brought the previous night when Michael called for food. As Michael handled the grill, everyone else sat all over on chairs or the railings of the balcony. Melody then hit her beer can several times and stated, "I have an announcement!"

"Here we go," Jim told the group with a grin.

Melody glared at Jim and repeated, "I have an announcement!" She went on to say, "As many of you know, I have only been in the service a little over five years. After careful consideration, I have decided to leave and retire early. I know, I know, I won't have my twenty in, but I have enough money to take it easy for a while and spend some time with three idiots in the woods." She laughed and looked at Alan.

"Three?" Alan said.

"Woof, woof," Melody said, and Alan suddenly appeared to understand.

"I need you all to understand," Melody told the group. "This is the best team I have ever seen. You work together more like a family than a unit, but I don't fit as well. Thank you for all you have done for me. I also considered asking to go back, but how could anything compare to what I have seen these past months? So, it is time to try something new." Melody looked over at Abby and said, "Thank you to all, but mostly you, Abby. Thank you for showing me and telling me how much someone can be loved and how much you love. After seeing it, I can do no less." Melody then put her arm around Alan.

The sun slowly started to set, and the entire group watched it together. They knew that tomorrow would be another day and they would be on the move once more.

About the Author

Andrew Allen Smith was born in Anderson, Indiana. Until the age of fifteen, he moved at least once per year and finally settled in Lexington, Kentucky. Andrew spent a significant amount of his teenage years reading and writing short stories, attempts at novels, and poetry. He published his first book, "A Slice of Passion," in 2005. It was a book of poetry compiled from dozens of years of work.

In 2015, Andrew published "The Theft and Other Short Stories" as a collection of some of his favorite portions of his writings after he was challenged to self-publish a book. Challenged and excited about his success, he published his first novel, "Vengeful Son," in 2016 and began building a franchise with that book. "The Masterson Files" (the series containing "Vengeful Son") now includes five books and has fifteen in outline form. The story follows an ex-assassin that is reluctantly engaged in helping others while trying to retire.

In 2020, after a tragic event, Andrew co-wrote "What NOT to Say to People Who Are Grieving." This book showcased emotions and an approach to helping others be more mindful of their words during grief.

2021 gave us "A Slice of Fear" followed by "Another Slice of Fear" with short stories focusing on fears of all types. "Another Slice of Fear" won Andrew a Literary Titan Award and has been reviewed positively for several stories in the genre.

As Quality Leader and System Architect, Andrew's work gave him credit for a series of instructional manuals for site relationship management systems, various quality documents, and development lifecycles. In Andrew's spare time, he has a passion for many hobbies and his family, which he considers paramount. For more information about Andrew, please visit **andrewallensmith.com**.

Books by Andrew Allen Smith

Fiction

A Slice of Passion

Another Slice of Passion

A Slice of Fear

Another Slice of Fear

Yet Another Slice of Fear

The Theft and Other Short Stories

The Masterson Files Series

Vengeful Son

Sinful Father

Deadly Daughter

Fateful Friend

Silent Sister

Curious Cousin

The Eternal Forever Series

Adam

Non-Fiction

What NOT to say to People Who are Grieving

Books Containing Andrew Allen Smith's prose

Monster Hunter Intern and Other Tales

The Gift and Other Stories

Simple Things: Moments of Isolated Gratitude

The Portrait of Herbert Losh and Other Stories

The Drifter and Other Unusual Tales

Quire

Coming Soon

Burial Ground

Stealth Drive

The Eternal Forever Book 2 – Morgan

www.ingramcontent.com/pod-product-compliance
Lightning Source LLC
Chambersburg PA
CBHW070750280626
47162CB00018B/2817